What are people saying about
Emjae Edwards' work?

Once again, Emjae Edwards has written a story that transports the reader into the minds, hearts, and locales of the characters. When you have finished 'Learning to be Irish', don't be surprised if you speak with a brogue (the accent, not the shoe) and bleed shamrocks. *More Books Please, Amazon reader*

Emjae Edwards takes us for a very exciting ride as we follow Garnet Steele from one coast to the other, trying to get her life back together after her first love goes very wrong. Highly recommended. *Kristie Leigh Maguire, Romance Author*

I really liked this story.This is the second book I've read by this author and what can I say but she is amazing at writing. *Nicky, Amazone reader*

Every once in a while Emjae amazes us with a turn of phrase that stuns us. We have to go back and read it again. For example: "Johnny Mathis' Chances Are melted out of the speaker." *Barbara Benson, Amazon reader*

You'll Wake Up One Morning
by
Emjae Edwards

Published
by
Inknbeans Press

Cover: Evonne

© December 2012 Emjae Edwards
and Inknbeans Press

ISBN-13: 978-0615758541 (Inknbeans
Press)
ISBN-10: 0615758541

Chapter One

The image was gripping: a lone man standing in the shadows below a dusty red sky, the eerie light of tracer fire arcing behind him, gunshots audible nearby. As the man talked, wind assailed him, snapping his dark blond hair into his eyes, sometimes hitting him with enough force to shift his position. Now and then artillery fire seemed so close the man flinched, but he never stopped talking, never surrendered his position.

In a room bathed in blue light, a half a world away, two young women watched these events, clinging to one another for support. The determined young man in the middle of the war zone was the only family these women had. He was Risë Mackie's brother and, for seven years, he had been Amanda Kraft's guardian, big brother and friend.

Gere Mackie was a lean, compact man, made leaner and more compact by the dark flak jacket he wore. As he addressed the camera, relating blow by blow the assault on the Embassy, barely visible behind him, something was taking place near enough to make the hands of the camera man tremble and Gere's image came back to that living room in San Francisco, shaking as if in the middle of an earthquake.

Tears slipped down Risë's face as she watched the scene. "I wish he hadn't gone," she wept.

"He couldn't stay home," Amanda soothed. "It's in his blood to be where the news is taking place." Amanda was the soother. It was her function in the family, but at that moment she wished for someone to comfort her. It was always beyond Risë's capabilities to recognize need in anyone else, but this situation would try the generosity of spirit in Mother Theresa.

"I know," Risë answered in a quaky voice, "but I still wish he hadn't gone."

"Me, too." Amanda tried to disengage herself from her friend, from the sofa and from the mesmerizing scene on the screen. She had to be at work in a few hours, but she had been riveted to the television since the siege began.

Gere had predicted this would take place when the US troops moved out. He had left for this tiny, embattled country three days ago, wanting to be on hand when things began to unfold. Even though analysts had discounted his beliefs, his network knew better and got him on a plane almost before he had finished presenting his request. He had an uncanny ability to see hot spots before they began to smolder, he saw flames when others were only just smelling smoke.

As he related details, his voice dropping to a cautious low, Gere was breaking the basic tenet of journalism: he was involved. But, at thirty three, he had already won a Pulitzer Prize for his inability to remain impartial. He had wept at the bedside of the dying, he had raised his voice against totalitarianism, he even gotten nose to nose with a U.S. Vice President over rising unemployment. To Gere Mackie, crime was wrong, sin was sin and anything that hurt children was abhorrent. Children were being turned into soldiers in that little part of the world and that, as anyone could see by the pain in Gere Mackie's face, was intolerable.

A rifle shot rang out so close that Gere ducked to one side, still talking, but a touch of anxiety crept into his voice.

"Oh, did you see that?" Risë cried, gripping Amanda's arm, pulling her down to the sofa at her side.

"He's fine," Amanda murmured, her heart in her throat. "Look at him. He's fine."

"I can't watch anymore." Risë jumped up from the sofa and paced, her back to the television, rubbing her arms nervously, peering over her shoulder every time her brother's hushed voice came through the speakers.

Amanda had to watch. They had been through this during the coups in Russia, the riots in Greece and France, the war in the Middle East. She should be used to it, she knew, but the idea of Gere being in danger was something she couldn't get used to. She tore her eyes from the screen to look up at Risë as she paced by. Oddly, she was struck by how similar these two were; dark blond, brown eyed, compact, athletic, filled with restless energy. There was no point in telling Risë to go to bed, just as there was no point in telling Gere to stay home. She looked at the television again.

Amanda had known Gere and Risë Mackie almost her entire life. Their fathers had been best friends in school. She and Risë had attended the same exclusive girls college in Santa Rosa, California. They both lost their mothers at a young age. Their fathers, both strong, successful, powerful men who loved to win, to be the best, had both died doing things they believed in.

Risë wanted to be wild. She had never really pursued a career after college. Despite Gere's nagging and Amanda's overzealous attempts to help, Risë had never found a job she could tolerate for more than a few weeks.

She was beautiful; a dainty woman with a soft voice and coquettish mannerisms, people often misapplied the 'dumb blonde' label. But she wasn't stupid, just easily bored. Consequently, she was seldom employed and devoted herself to shopping and flirting and partying. Yet, even then she couldn't devote enough focus to be truly bad.

Gere was just the opposite in temperament. Amanda recalled hearing her father say more than once that Gere ought to have been his son. He was hard working and disciplined, driven to achieve and hyper focused. But Gere despised the military, and Amanda's highly decorated and combat hardened father was an anathema to a young man dedicated to reporting the facts.

Gere had been only eighteen when he assumed responsibility for his sister when their father died. A couple of years later he petitioned for guardianship of Amanda rather than have her become a ward of the state when her own father died. He never claimed to be a good parent – he didn't try to be one. He only endeavored to keep the two girls warm and fed and out of jail. Somehow he managed to keep an eye on them, get through college and get a job at a local television station, where he started his career doing weekend sports reports.

Occasionally, he'd be assigned to cover for a vacationing anchor, and there Gere Mackie began to shine. Ratings soared when he was on the desk. Women tuned in because he was a good looking young man with dimples and a winning smile. Men liked that he didn't just play on his looks, that he could report the news intelligently without giving sway to the happy talk trend.

It didn't take long for the nation to get a look at him. Within a year, Gere was offered a network position, on assignment all over California, and then all over the country and, at last, the world. Once Amanda and Risë left for college, Gere lobbied for and won a position in the Middle East. He was thrilled, calling it the assignment of a lifetime.

It was a short lifetime. Something happened there. Amanda and Risë never knew what it was, but Gere came home abruptly, a little different, withdrawn and saddened, a little disappointed by his fellow men.

This was the first time he had taken a foreign assignment in two years and listening to sounds of battle around him, Amanda was starting to fear it might be his last. Voice rising to be heard over the gunfire, his eyes darting to the right, Gere very abruptly sent the feed back to the newsroom in New York.

Risë returned to the sofa, settling down close to Amanda, grasping her hand. The man at the desk began recapping what Gere had said, a map of the area superimposed behind his head.

Amanda sighed and struggled with a yawn. "Look," she said, indicating the clock on the map, "over there the day's just ended. That same day starts for us in a couple of hours. It's like looking into the future."

"He shouldn't have gone," Risë repeated, squeezing Amanda's fingers. "Something terrible is going to happen."

Amanda felt a chill ripple over her spine. Risë had said that on two other occasions: the weekend before her father died and when Gere was on assignment in New England. The helicopter he was riding in crashed in a remote mountain area and he was given up for lost in the bad weather and rough terrain. Six days later, he walked out of the woods on a tree limb made into a splint for his broken leg. The newsman had become the news.

She risked a glance at Risë. "What do you mean?"

Risë shook her head, her brow wrinkling up in a determined frown. "I don't know. I just have that feeling." She focused on Amanda. "You know, that awful feeling."

"Shh," Amanda soothed at the first sparkle of tears in Risë's eyes. "Stop thinking that way. You know Gere's going to call any moment and tell us not to worry. Just wait."

They sat together in silence, watching the blue light of the television flicker before them, neither seeing nor hearing a thing. Every nerve, every sense was waiting for the chirp of Risë's phone on the table

But it was silent, too.

At some point in their fruitless vigil Risë fell asleep, her head weighing heavily on Amanda's shoulder. As the sun rose and cast a grey light into the room, Amanda was grateful that Risë wasn't awake. The coverage of the events had taken an alarming turn as the broadcasters in New York began to cautiously address Gere's abrupt termination of his report, the firefight that was obviously close enough to alarm him, and the fact that he had not responded to any further attempts to contact him.

Amanda shut off the television at seven o'clock and Risë sat up sharply. "What happened? Did Gere call?"

She was tempted to lie. Instead, she put on a brave smile and stood. "Not yet. He probably didn't want to wake us. I'll go put a kettle on and then I must take a shower and get ready for work. I'm going to be late if I don't rush."

Risë laughed grimly. "Oh, Amanda, it is never more obvious that you had an English nanny than when we're in crisis. Your solution to everything is to make tea."

"Well, it makes more sense than pacing, wringing your hands and making dire predictions." She bit her lip. She hadn't meant to rebuke Risë for her worry. It was natural and more justified than she yet knew. She patted Risë's shoulder. "He'll be okay, Risë. He's a survivor."

Risë nodded, but her lower lip was trembling and her brown eyes were glossy with tears. "I guess you think I'm overreacting."

"Not at all-"

"But he's all I've got!-"

Amanda glanced away. "He's all I've got, too," she murmured. Risë never deliberately did it, but somehow she always managed to remind Amanda that she was an outsider, not really a part of the family, that she shared this huge, three bedroom apartment on Jackson Street with the Mackies on their sufferance only, and any time they felt they had completed their obligation to her, she would be out on the street with nowhere to go and belonging to no one.

Risë was too lost in fear to realize what she had done. She began to pace again.

Amanda left her and went into the kitchen, to be English, to put the kettle on.

Amanda had always liked the Mackie kitchen. It was large and warm and homey and, as long as she had lived with them, it had been the hub of family life. Upon becoming head of the household, Gere had learned to cook and every evening, no matter what his schedule, if the girls were not away at school, Gere found time to prepare a meal for them. It might not have been *haute cuisine* but it was nourishing. The only time the three of them had taken a vacation together, it had been planned around that big chrome and tile kitchen table. Amanda and Risë hunched over a dozen college applications, trying to decide where they wanted to attend, with Gere hovering over them, trying to be encouraging and at the same time discouraging any suggestion of a campus too far away. To Amanda, the brown and yellow tiles of this room signified home.

She filled the kettle and put it on the stove, flipping the knob to start the fire, and counting to six as she always did before the gas ignited a strong blue flame. As the water came to a boil, she prowled the cupboards for something to nibble with the tea. What would she do if she was no longer a part of the Mackie household? What if Gere didn't come back? Would Risë completely fall apart or would she reveal a solid steel spine of her own? It was hard to imagine Risë taking charge the way her brother had. This was a woman whose brother had to hold her hand and reassure her all the way down to campus the first six Mondays after college began, because every Friday she would come home in tears, determined not to go back. This was a woman with two degrees in chemistry, who always took jobs as a secretary or waitress because she was afraid of the challenges in her own field. This was a woman who couldn't sustain a relationship; either she dated men who expected her to contribute to the decision making process, and got impatient when she didn't, or she dated the type of man who took advantage of weak willed women. Either way she would end up crying. And either way, she forced Gere to assume that not so coveted role of big brother and chase the offender off.

At least Amanda had never put him through that, a fact she secretly both deplored and took pride in. She had so immersed herself in her studies that she seldom had time for dates. And now that she had a place (a low one) in a prestigious law firm, all she focused on was survival.

Amanda had a horrible thought just as the kettle began to scream. What if, in the event of Gere's...(she couldn't even let herself *think* the word) Risë expected her to take charge?

"You're scared, too."

Amanda turned sharply, splashing boiling water on the brown and yellow tiles. "What are you talking about?"

Risë was standing in the doorway, her hands braced against the frame to keep herself upright. "You can't lie to me." She wavered in the doorway. "I saw your face just now. You're scared, too." Her face pinched up and her voice quavered. "What will we do if he...if he-"

"Don't say it," Amanda commanded. She brought two oversized brown cups of sweetened tea to the table. "In the first place, he's not going to. Gere's got more lives than a whole litter of kittens. And, in the second place, no matter what happens, one of these days we're going to have to learn to survive on our own. He's not going what to look after us forever." She shrugged. "Suppose he decides to get married? Do you think he and his wife will adopt us?"

Risë slid down into a chair, momentarily distracted by the argument. "Don't you think it's odd that he hasn't?" she mused.

Amanda shrugged again. She'd never given his romantic life any thought. "No, not really."

Risë stirred her tea, a thoughtful frown replacing the worried wrinkle. "Just think about it for a minute. He's thirty three years old. He's good looking and famous." She toyed with her spoon. "But he never dates the same girl more than a few times."

Amanda opened a box of cookies. "He's probably just not ready to settle down." She pushed the box toward Risë. "Why should he? He can have any woman he wants just by smiling." It was strange to think of Gere in these terms. She would never think of her father this way. What if Gere did want to settle down? He wouldn't want his sister hanging around. He certainly wouldn't want a pseudo sister in the way.

Risë nibbled nervously on the edge of a shortbread. "I think he met someone when he was in Saudi Arabia," she said.

Amanda didn't want to entertain such an idea but the topic was keeping Risë from her near paralyzing fear. "Why do you say that? What did he tell you?"

Risë put the half eaten cookie down and wiped the corners of her mouth with her fingertips. "He never *said* anything," she answered, "but he brought back a photograph."

"He brought back tons of photographs." Amanda reached for her tea. "He always does."

"He didn't put this one away in a photo album like he always does." Risë stood. "Come with me."

"Risë, I don't have time for this. I need to be at work in-"

"Just come on."

Mystified and curious, Amanda rose and followed Risë down the hall to the bedroom that had once belonged to Risë's parents. She stalled at the sill. As long as she had lived in that apartment, Gere's room had always been off limits, but Risë sailed in, showing no remorse for violating his privacy. She went right to the bedside table and rifled through drawers.

Amanda took a moment to look around. The room was definitely Gere's: Spartan and efficient, a dark wood double bed, a large clean desk, a small bureau, a stationary bike, a small trophy case where his little league trophies had as much prominence as his

Pulitzer. A wedding picture of his parents was the only photograph visible.

"Here." Risë sat down on the bed, a small white bundle in her hands. It was a handkerchief with a grey monogrammed GFM. Risë and Amanda had saved up and sent away to Sulka's to get a dozen of them for his twenty first birthday. "Look at this."

Amanda sat down beside her and accepted the first photograph. It was a very pretty Middle Eastern girl; long black hair, large expressive brown eyes, flashing white teeth showing in what seemed to be a titillated yet furtive smile. Around her throat, her fingers clenched dark cloth as if she had removed her head scarf only long enough for one photograph.

"I've never seen these two." Risë held them up, the top one showed a crowd of veiled women, all walking away from the camera, except for one small figure glancing back. Amanda knew she was being fanciful but she thought she saw longing in the young woman's eyes. When Risë tucked that photo behind the other, she gasped.

When Amanda looked at the third photo, she gasped, too. It was a photo of a baby, wrapped in blue cloth, with large dark eyes and curly blond hair.

Amanda, drowning in guilt, took the photos and wrapped them up again. "Now we know why he doesn't get involved with other women." She shoved the bundle back into the drawer. "Shame on you for looking at them."

Risë ignored her. "Gere's a father," she breathed, stunned. "He has a child." She looked up at the wall, blinking quickly. "He must be two or five by now. "

"Don't start dwelling on it. We're not supposed to know anything about it." Amanda started for the door. "I've got to get ready for work."

"I wonder if Gere has any contact with that girl or the baby."

Amanda tugged at her sleeve. "That's something we'll never know. Now, let's get out of here."

"I'm going to ask him the next time I talk to him," Risë announced.

"You're not!" Amanda protested, horrified.

"Why not? I think I have a right to know." Risë pressed a fist to her breast. "I am his sister."

"You invaded his privacy, you don't have any rights," Amanda argued, shrilly. "If he had wanted us to know, he would have told us."

"Oh, you're sounding like a lawyer again." Risë brushed Amanda's hands away. "This is above the law."

"Nothing is above the law, Risë," Amanda countered stiffly. Now that she was back in the hallway she felt a little better, but only a little. Gere had left a child behind in the Saudi desert. Why did *she* feel betrayed?

Amanda's position at Bond, Walker & Phills was little more than glorified chair filler. Even though her business cards identified her as an attorney, she had yet to provide any more assistance than as 'third chair' in the courtroom. In the offices, she was the go-to researcher and she was generally regarded as a hard worker, but no one really believed she would ever be a litigator. Amanda, in her heart, wasn't that sure she wanted to litigate. Her father, a career Army officer, had made it clear that she had to distinguish herself in some profession. She didn't have the stamina for the military, or the stomach for medicine, making law the only obvious choice. Amanda, in her heart, wanted to be a musician.

On that morning, however, she was glad to be a cog in the grinding wheel of justice. It kept her mind occupied. Since few people knew of her relationship to Gere Mackie, she was able to keep her thoughts focused on *Nierny v. Chafta Health Care*. She stayed out of the conference room, where she knew there would be a television set on twenty four hour news, and kept her contact with co-workers to a minimum to avoid being drawn into a conversation about the news of the day.

She was doing all right until she returned from lunch to find her supervisor waiting in her cubical. "There are some men to see you," he said gravely.

"Me? Why?" Amanda put her purse in a drawer and straightened her twin set cardigan. "Who are they?"

He nodded toward Mr. Bond's office, one of six which surrounded the sea of cubicles. "They say they're from the State Department."

"The State- oh, it's a mistake. They must be looking for someone else."

He shook his head. "No, they were pretty definite it was you that they wanted."

She rubbed her aching brow. "It must have something to do with Gere. My...my roommate's brother." She realized she was trembling and didn't even try to rally her nerves. The State Department could only mean one thing: one very bad thing. "Where are they?"

"In Mr. Bond's office. You know, Ms. Kraft, we don't like unflattering attention from the government or media."

"Nor do I. This has nothing to do with me. I'm only on the periphery, I assure you." She tugged at her cardigan again. "Let's go."

Two men were sitting at the table next to the windows in Mr. Bond's office. They could have come off an assembly line that morning; both were probably not a fraction over or under six feet tall, their suits were the same shade of grey, they both had the same short, no nonsense haircut although one's hair was black and the other brown, even their expression of concern was identical.

Mr. Bond was sitting behind his desk looking uncomfortable, but he forced a smile and stood when she entered. "This is Miss Kraft. Now, before I leave you, does Miss Kraft require legal representation?"

Both men stood, belatedly, shaking their heads as they offered their credentials revealing that their names were Mr. Pope and Mr. Peterson. "This isn't an investigation, Mr. Bond, merely a fact finding inquiry. Thank you for your cooperation. Miss Kraft?" One of them indicated a chair.

Amanda smiled tightly at the senior partner and then, smoothing her skirt, settled into a chair. "What is this all about?"

Apparently Mr. Pope was taking point on the conversation for he fired his first question before either of them were seated. "How are you related to Gere Mackie?"

Her heart lurched, and she actually sat forward before she forced herself to sit back and at least attempt to appear calm. "I'm not related to him, that is, I am not a blood relative. Why are you on a fact finding inquiry about Mr. Mackie, and how can anything I say be relevant?" She noticed that Mr. Bond was lingering at the door, and she felt her cheeks getting hot in embarrassment.

Mr. Pope looked at Mr. Peterson and then looked at Amanda. "We're talking to anyone who might have had recent contact with Mr. Mackie."

She looked toward the door again. Mr. Bond saw her very direct look and slipped out the door. "The last time I spoke to him was Tuesday evening."

Mr. Peterson was writing something in a notepad as Mr. Pope continued. "What was the nature of your conversation?"

"He was preparing to leave on assignment." She held her breath for a moment so it wouldn't tremble. "Perhaps if you told me what facts you were trying to find, I could better answer your questions."

They ignored her suggestion. "Did he say where he was being assigned?"

"Yes. Near Somalia."

They looked at one another again, brows lifting slightly as if she'd said something significant. Mr. Peterson wrote quickly. Mr. Pope said, "Did he indicate what his plans were?"

"To report the news. What else would a reporter plan to do?"

He folded his hands in front of him. "What news was he planning to report?"

"The assault of the Embassy, I suppose." She fluttered one hand nervously. "This is very-"

"That did not occur until Wednesday evening," Mr. Pope interrupted. "Why did he leave Tuesday?"

"I don't know." She thought for a moment. "You're not suggesting that he had something to do with it, are you?"

"We're not suggesting anything," he denied quickly. He consulted with Mr. Peterson via another raised brow. "We're just trying to find out if he had some sort of advance knowledge, some contact there who might have warned him it was going to happen."

"I think if you look at Mr. Mackie's record you'll find he's very intuitive."

Amanda wanted to squirm in her chair, but if she had learned one thing during her time at Bond, Walker and Phills it was how to appear impassive despite the circumstances.

"So, you're saying he had no contacts in the area."

"Not to my knowledge."

"How intimate is your knowledge?" he asked.

Amanda looked at him, sharply. "I beg your pardon?"

"How well do you know him?" he persisted.

"I've known him all my life. He's a family friend." This is bad, she thought. This is very, very bad. Something's happened to Gere, something bad enough that the State Department is involved.

"You live in his house." There was no change of inflection in his voice, yet Amanda perceived the tiniest accusation in the statement.

She narrowed her eyes. "It appears you've done a lot of fact finding already. Yes, I share the apartment with Mr. Mackie and his sister."

The accusation was clearer now. "So, you're denying any relationship with Mr. Mackie?"

"No, I'm denying the kind of relationship you're insinuating," she answered coolly. "Mr. Mackie was my legal guardian after my father died."

Mr. Peterson opened a manila folder and pushed it toward her interrogator. He studied and looked up. "Your father was Major Walter Kraft?"

She felt her throat tightened. "Yes."

"And he died in Iraq?"

"Yes." It was barely a whisper.

"We're very sorry for your loss."

Oh, she was so tired of that rote phrase. "Thank you."

Mr. Pope put the folder aside. "How did it happen that Mr. Mackie became your guardian? You must have had other relatives?"

She sat back in the chair, folding her hands before her, very primly. "Mr. Mackie's father and my father were very good friends, going back to their time at West Point. Mr. Mackie's father married a woman who disliked the military, and so they fell out for many years. After Mrs. Mackie passed away unexpectedly, they reestablished contact and Mr. Mackie's father married my mother's cousin, although their marriage was short lived as the second Mrs. Mackie was diagnosed with cancer shortly after the birth of their daughter. Mr. Mackie's father died on an expedition to the Andes, and because my mother was related to their daughter, she looked after Mr. Mackie and his sister until she d-died," she paused and coughed slightly, "at which time Mr. Mackie sought to be made his sister's guardian. A few years later, my father was killed in action. I had no living relatives, so in return for my mother's care when they were younger, Mr. Mackie sought to be made my guardian as well." She met their eyes, impassively. "That's how it happened that he became my guardian, and what my relationship with both of the Mackies is to this day. Now, will you please tell me what this is all about?"

"Does Mr. Mackie have any other relatives?"

For a moment, Amanda considered the photograph of that beautiful baby. "None of which I am aware."

The two men huddled for a moment. "Miss Kraft, our sources have indicated that Mr. Mackie may have been taken hostage during this unfortunate event at the Embassy."

Amanda shut her eyes and pressed a fist to her mouth. When she opened her eyes, she said, "You mean, he might be dead."

They weren't prepared to admit that. "We had hoped to develop other possible scenarios such meeting with a contact or relative in the area."

"He wouldn't do that."

"How can you be so confident?"

"Well, for one thing, he went there to report on the situation, and that assault on the Embassy is an ongoing story. There is no way he would go visiting friends and family while there was breaking news right under his nose. For another thing, if he felt he had reported all he could and wanted to get out of the area, he would have come back here. He would have at least contacted one of us, and we haven't heard from him."

It was obvious from their stony expressions that they had come to that conclusion before they arrived at Bond, Walker and Phills. "Thank you for your time, Miss Kraft." They stood together, and each offered a hand. "We'll be in touch."

"Wait." She stood up, too. "What's being done to find him?"

"If we have any information we can disseminate we'll contact you."

"What do you know right now?"

They ignored her, walking out, shoulder to shoulder.

Amanda wanted to fling herself face forward on the table, and sob into her hands, but that was neither the time nor place. Instead, she stood, smoothed her hair back and straightened her skirt, lifted her chin and left the office.

Chapter Two

Amanda stepped off the bus at the corner, took a deep breath of salty air, and looked down the street. Today it seemed miles from the bus stop to the yellow and white Victorian style building she called home. It had been such a difficult afternoon. Everyone in the office was talking about the conflict, but no one seemed to sympathize with the fact that she knew someone who was right in the middle of it all.

It was a big office but everywhere she went she encountered reminders. Everyone was talking about the visit from the State Department without considering all the implications. The television in the conference room was kept on, with the volume high, and people were gathered around the table watching whenever they were free, and those in their cubicles tweeted, chatted and commented on Facebook about the fact that three reporters and a cameraman had disappeared. Once again the newsman had become the news.

As she dragged herself up the sidewalk, she dreaded what she might find at home. Surely Mr. Pope and Mr. Peterson had gone to the house first, and no doubt upset Risë. The fact that Risë hadn't phoned or texted her immediately after their visit was doubly worrisome. Risë couldn't make a sandwich without telling someone about it. Surely a visit from two representatives of the State Department warranted a text.

When she reached the house, she paused, staring up at the bay windows of the front room, looking for some sign of Risë. The window was dark. Sighing, she climbed the stairs and unlocked the foyer door. On the floor, in the middle of worn carpet, was a business card which must have been stuffed through the old mail slot. She picked it up, and held it up to catch the light of the street lamp outside.

Mr. Peterson of the State Department.

She tucked the card into her bag and started to climb the stairs, her heart a fraction lighter. So, they hadn't spoken to Risë. She would take small mercies wherever they came.

Upstairs, the apartment was cold and chaotic. It was evident that Risë had gone on some kind of frenzy. Cabinets had been opened, drawers searched, cushions over turned. Amanda might have feared that the house had been burgled, or that the State Department had invited themselves in for a little look around, but she had seen Risë do this before; once, having lost a ring, she turned the whole place upside down, including Amanda's room, convinced it might have gotten caught on a shoe or trouser hem and carried off.

Amanda wandered around the front room for a moment, taking in the clutter, then shrugged out of her coat, and went into the kitchen to clear a path for preparing dinner.

She was not a great cook, but she could manage more than take out and pizza deliveries, which seemed to be Risë's best. On the other hand, Risë had exquisite taste for the presentation of formal meals, did an excellent job of matching wines, and knew every fine restaurant in the Bay Area. Between the two of them, even when Gere was away, they never went hungry.

She was stirring gravy into steamed rice when she heard the door open downstairs. She did not hear Risë's usual dash up the stairs, but someone was coming up, slowly and heavily. Could it be Gere? Before she could turn down the fire and wipe her hands, someone came through the door, rustling bags, and sighing, "What a mess."

"Risë?" Amanda stepped around the corner. Risë looked exhausted and bedraggled, two things she never allowed herself to be. From her hands dangled a bag from the corner grocer and a bag full of books. "What's this?"

"Sorry about all this." Risë sagged against the doorframe. "I meant to get home before you and get it all cleaned up. I was going to fix dinner, too." She straightened up and held out the bag of food. "Penne pasta with chicken breasts and a salad. I didn't think I could mess that up too much. Oh, well," she sighed, "it can keep for tomorrow."

Amanda took the bag and carried it into the kitchen. "What happened here?"

"Oh, I don't know." Risë let her coat slide from her shoulders and then slung it over the back of the sofa. "I guess I just started...panicking. What if Gere doesn't come home?"

"He will." Amanda began to empty the bag.

"But what if he didn't? How could we survive?"

"We just would." Wine, pasta, pesto sauce in a jar, a bag of greens...no chicken, of course. It was too much to hope she'd remember everything. "And he will come home."

"Oh, easy for you, Miss Trust Fund." Risë dropped her purse on the table. "All I've got is this apartment, and who knows what that's worth these days." She pulled a chair out and dropped into it, covering her face. "I've got to get a job. I went out looking for one today. But then I ended up in a book store, buying all these 'how to get a job in today's economy' type books. Mmm, that smells good."

"It wouldn't hurt you to get a job, if for no other reason than to get you past these panic fits you have," Amanda told her, putting the wine into the rack. "And he *will* come back." She wondered if she said it enough it could be true.

"Of course he will," Risë said without conviction.. "I don't suppose you heard anything today?"

Amanda was tempted, once again, to lie. "Well, it depends. I didn't hear from Gere, but I did have visitors at the office." She lifted the lid off the pan of rice and stirred again. "Two men from the State Department. They asked a lot of questions." She nodded toward the door. "They came here, too, evidently. There was a card in the door."

"State Department," Risë breathed. "What did they…" her eyes got very large, and started to sparkle with tears. "He *is* dead."

"No, he's just out of communication," Amanda clarified. "They think he went to some friends or contacts in the area."

"He doesn't have any."

"That we know about," she countered. "Anyway, they promised to keep us up to date." Well, that *was* a lie, but it was their lie, not hers.

Risë covered her face with her hands again, and for a moment her shoulders shuddered, and she made tiny, wheezing sounds like wind through a cracked window, but she recovered quickly and sat very straight, wiping away tears. "I'm sorry. I'm just exhausted."

"Of course you are."

Risë stood again and looked around. "Let me go change, and I'll clean this up."

Amanda answered with a nod and turned her attention to the mushrooms and peppers waiting to be chopped.

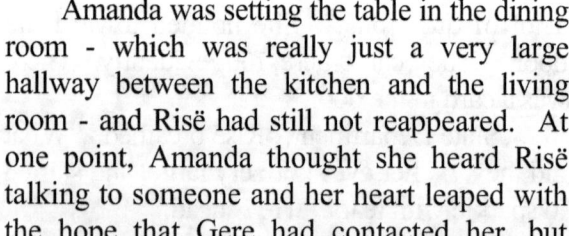

Amanda was setting the table in the dining room - which was really just a very large hallway between the kitchen and the living room - and Risë had still not reappeared. At one point, Amanda thought she heard Risë talking to someone and her heart leaped with the hope that Gere had contacted her, but when there was no joyful whoop, and Risë did not appear, smiling broadly, she gave up that hope.

Bringing napkins to the table, the last step before serving the food, she called out to Risë. Getting no response, she peered down the hallway to the door at the end. There was a sliver of light beneath the door unbroken by the shadows of a person moving around inside. No sound drifted toward her. She went to the door and tapped. "Risë? Dinner's on the table." There was still no response.

She eased the door open.

Risë, still in a bathrobe, her golden hair wrapped in a pink towel, was stretched across her bed, her phone in hand.

Sighing, Amanda came fully into the room, picked up the quilt Risë's mother had made for her, and draped it over her friend's shoulders. She eased the phone from Risë's fingers, noting that she had not made or accepted a single call in eighteen hours, letting everything go to voice mail. She wasn't going to risk missing Gere's call. "That's the spirit," Amanda whispered. "Don't give up hope." She put the phone on the bedside table, turned out the light, and went back to the kitchen to put dinner away.

The twenty four hour news programs were still full of the coup, and Gere's name and image featured prominently. She didn't even have to turn on the sound to know that they were replaying his last broadcast words again and again, showing clips of him flinching and glancing to his left. She flipped to other channels for distraction, but she wasn't interested in expensive cars, remodeling houses or watching men swear in restaurant kitchens. She got up, made herself a sandwich and came back to watch the news again.

There was very little being reported she didn't already know, but she could not bring herself to stop watching. It would be like abandoning Gere in his hour of need. She had to watch. She had to be there when there was something new to learn.

She got up and rinsed the sandwich plate, wiped down the countertops, put the white lace tablecloth back on the dining room table, closed cupboards and drawers, righted chairs, and put cushions back where they belonged. She sorted newspapers, magazines and mail that had been scattered across the floor. She got out the carpet broom and ran it over the ancient Oriental rug in front of the television. Every action was punctuated with an affirmation that Gere would come home soon.

She made tea and stared out the window at the City, which insisted on sparkling like stars without a care in the world. She pushed a window open and listened to the traffic, the voices, the music, the ding-ding of cable cars a few blocks away. She lingered there in the normalcy of the outside world, and wished with all her heart that Gere was home to make her world normal again.

She thought about the baby in the photo Risë had shown her. It didn't look like Gere. Then again, it didn't not look like him. It looked exactly the way a baby ought to look if his mother was from Iraq and his father wasn't. Who was this girl? In the photo she looked very young, perhaps too young. She couldn't imagine Gere getting involved with an underaged girl. Well, she couldn't imagine Gere getting involved with anyone…except his viewers. He was always so earnest, so involved, so intimate with his viewers, one could almost imagine him sitting across the dinner table reporting on the end of the world.

Or maybe that was just her perspective. After all, she did hear him reporting on the end of the world from the other side of the table all the time. That voice determined to be heard over the roar of iniquity was genuine. There was nothing contrived about him.

Shutting out the image of him on television she thought back to the day she had come into this apartment to stay. She had known Risë all her life, their mothers had been so close, and then Risë had stayed with Amanda and her family during the week, and going home on weekends, after her mother died. Gere was in school then, so she didn't see much of him, but Risë spoke of him constantly, so she knew a lot about him.

Then her own mother died, and shortly after her father was killed in action. She was being moved to a foster family when Gere made a call. And the next thing she knew she was coming into the apartment, not as a guest, but as a part of the family. Risë had met her with a hug, talking fast and loud and punctuated with giggles. Behind her, Gere stood leaning in that doorway between the living room and dining room, arms folded over his chest. He looked so young. He was barely twenty then. He saw her looking at him and he straightened and spread his arms, inviting her into the shelter of his care.

She pulled the window shut and looked back to that place where he had been standing that day, wondering if she'd ever see him there again.

That night turned into another day, another night. The days and nights became a week and then a month. Risë went through phases of hope, panic, anger and apathy. Amanda worked. She did not hear from Mr. Pope or Mr. Peterson again, and gradually other events overtook the news broadcasts. Some days Gere and his colleagues did not even get a mention.

Risë got a job at the book store when she took all those books back, and she managed to keep the position for over a month. When she wasn't working, however, she was tearing the apartment apart as if looking for something.

Amanda would come home each night not knowing what she would find. Some nights the house would be pristine, some nights it was a mess but a fine meal had been prepared, and some nights it was just a disaster, and Risë would meet her at the door, purse and coat in hand, ready to go out for a meal.

Neither woman dated during that horrible period. No man had anything to offer that could help them escape their fear and doubt, and the growing belief that that Gere was dead. Risë didn't even take calls from her girlfriends. When Amanda was home she saw that Risë was either in front of the television or in front of the computer.

The day he'd been gone a week, Risë was convinced he was dead and they were about to be flung out on the street. The next day she went through Gere's bedroom, presumably looking for a will. When he'd been missing a month, she was bright and upbeat, convinced that he would be back any day, and insisted that she and Amanda go out and get haircuts and manicures to look their best when he returned. The next day she stayed in bed, sobbing.

Amanda was starting to crumble around the edges. She couldn't keep up with Risë's mood swings and ideas. She couldn't keep the house clean, and meals cooked and be Risë's analyst much longer. She felt as if she'd aged a year for every day he'd been gone.

Then came the awful day when the news broke about a grave discovered about a mile from the Embassy. No details were given other than the fact that the bodies were probably European or American. Barely choking back panic of her own, Amanda sought permission to leave the office early, and hurried home, hoping Risë hadn't heard yet.

Risë wasn't home, or if she was, she wasn't answering the door. A half dozen news vans were lined up, illegally parked and making the one way street impassable. Satellite antennas towered over the vans, people with video cameras and microphones were standing around, dragging cables and power cords over the sidewalk and street. Amanda knew she did not want to climb the steps to her house and be bombarded with questions. She retraced her steps, went around the corner to the alley and peered down the passageway. There was no sign of anyone lingering there.

Passing the first house, as she picked her way down the alley in the falling light, Amanda had the eerie feeling she was being watched, but she had seen no one in the passage. Pausing at the next fence, she looked up and scanned the windows of houses looking into the alley. There were no lights showing, no faces visible, no shadows, not even the fluttering of a curtain. As she reached the gate behind her building, she felt a hand on her shoulder and she nearly screamed.

"Shh," Risa warned, pulling her into the concrete walkway behind the gate. "We've got to get out of here. There are hundreds of reporters out front."

"I know," Amanda began. "Why do you think I'm back here?"

Risë ignored the question, and rose up on tip toe to peer over the fence. "I assumed you got my message."

"No, I…" Amanda pulled her phone out of her briefcase. There was a text from Risë sent only a few moments before. "Do you know why they're here?"

"I have no idea." Risë dropped down again. "It looks clear. Let's go."

"Where are we going?" Amanda demanded as Risë tugged at her arm, hunching down as she scurried back to the street.

"I don't know," Risë panted when they reached the sidewalk. "Anywhere but here. I just can't face reporters."

"They may not want to talk to us," Amanda pointed out, straining to keep up with Risë. "I heard someone won the big lottery last night. You know how Mrs. Cleary is always playing the lottery."

"Hmm, maybe." Risë stopped at the streetlight, considered it and discarded it before the light changed. "I don't feel like taking the chance. Do you?"

"No," Amanda sighed, being pulled along. "I suppose not." She actually thought the idea that their downstairs neighbor had some good luck might be valid. After all, she hadn't heard from Mr. Pope or Mr. Peterson, and wouldn't they come calling if they thought Gere was…no, she still wasn't ready to say it. "I hope Mrs. Cleary did win. She could use the money."

Risë pointed to a coffee shop on the next block, and Amanda nodded. If nothing else, it would be good to be out of the house for a while.

They ordered their drinks and took a table at the back of the shop. Risë settled in, shaking packets of pink stuff. "How did you get here so fast? I didn't expect to see you for hours."

Amanda worked the lid off her cup of tea and swished the bag around with a plastic stirring stick. "I was already on my way home."

"Why? You never leave early. It's a miracle when you leave on time." Risë began emptying the pink packets into her cup.

"I…um…" Amanda wondered if she was up to dealing with Risë's reaction if she truly didn't know what had been discovered. "I felt like coming home. I was tired."

"Yes. You look tired. Poor thing." Risë reached across the table, impulsively. "You're taking this so hard. Anyone would think you'd lost your brother, too."

Amanda bit down on her lower lip. "Yes, I suppose they might," she said in a low voice.

Risë was quiet for a moment. "I'm sorry. I suppose he is like a brother to you, isn't he?"

"Well," she exhaled on a shudder, "he is the nearest thing for me."

"How do people stand not having any family at all?"

"It isn't easy," Amanda admitted.

"You've got family!" Risë said, indignantly. "You have us."

Amanda looked up, surprised. That was probably the nicest and most unexpected thing she had ever heard Risë say. "Thank you."

"I'm surprised you didn't know," Risë continued, pouring another packet of sweetener into her cup. "Gere's always doted on you."

"Has he?" Amanda felt her cheeks getting a little warm.

"Oh, good grief, yes." Risë sipped her coffee, made a face and reached for more pink packets. "He always brags about how smart and steady you are."

"Steady?" That wasn't exactly flattering, Amanda thought. Risë's beautiful and charming and has style. Next to her 'steady' is nothing.

"Oh, yes. Dependable. Honest. Trustworthy." She rolled her eyes. "He goes on and on about you."

"Too bad I'm not a Labrador Retriever."

Risë missed the implication. "He says your word as like gold. You're honest even when it hurts. You're serious. He never has to worry about you doing something foolish or acting silly."

"No," Amanda said. She was sure Gere meant the comments to be favorable but hearing Risë tick them off made her sound boring and unattractive. Who would be interested in a 'steady' woman?

"Whereas me, on the other hand..." Risë rolled her eyes. "I swear, I think he expects me to bring down a government every time I step out the door."

"Have you brought down many governments lately?" Amanda wound the string to her teabag around the stirrer and lifted it from the cup.

"Not in years." Risë giggled. "Boy, you cause one country to overthrow its dictator and they never let you…" she let it go, her lower lip quivering.

Amanda patted her hand, gently. "He'll be back, Risë. You'll see."

She nodded, but her lip continued to quiver.

They sat quietly for a while, both lost in memories. Amanda thought of her mother, a forceful, no nonsense woman who thought she could push through anything, including cancer. She and her father had been a match; a soft, retiring woman such as Risë's mother would have been steamrolled by her father's personality. Amanda thought about Risë's description of her and wondered if she had inherited some of her mother's qualities. She certainly didn't have her mother's charm and warm heart. If she did, maybe Gere would have used something besides 'steady' to describe her.

Perhaps she was steady. She certainly never caught the attention of the kind of man she wanted: a daredevil with a twinkling eye and boyish grin. She wanted the kind of man who would provide her with adventure. Or a man with a musical gift that defied explanation, who could transport her to worlds unseen. She wanted a man like Gere and Amanda's father, who loved adventure and was passionate about art and music. Of course, he hadn't come to a good end, so her ideal man must have some sense and reason, as well. Such a man didn't exist, and if he did, he'd be captivated by someone as sparkling as Risë, not a steady woman like herself.

Risë swished the remaining coffee around in her cup, looking as if her thoughts were resting on some distant planet but Amanda knew better. Risë wasn't a deep thinker, her mind was always on the here and now, with a healthy dose of what if sprinkled in. She could, simultaneously, worry about Gere's fate, consider painting the powder room pink, wonder what they would have for supper and wish she had a new pair of boots – all while trying to decide if she wanted a second coffee. Finally, she took a sip and put the cup down. "Why did you come home early, Amanda? Do you know something…something that would make reporters come to our door?"

Amanda put down her cup, too. She wondered if she should insist that they go home before she revealed the news, but perhaps being in a public place would force Risë to contain her emotions until she had time to reflect on them. "Risë, haven't you listened to the news at all today?"

Risë shook her head, looking frightened. "No, there hasn't been any news about him for so long…"

"Well, this might not be about him, either, so keep that in mind. There was a grave discovered-"

Risë made a little 'eeep' sound, and she covered her mouth with both hands as everyone else in the crowded shop turned to look at her.

"Now, now listen to me." Amanda put her hand on Risë's arm. "There was a grave, but no one's been identified. So it's very possible that it has nothing…what are you doing?"

Risë was emptying her cup, and standing, gathering her purse and coat. "I have to go home. If something happens, if they find out anything, how will they know how to find us and tell us?" She tugged at Amanda's hand. "Come on. Let's go."

"But…but the reporters."

"I don't care about them. Let's go." She pushed her way through people queuing up around the register, leaving Amanda to trail along behind, issuing apologies.

Even as they hurried down the traffic lined street, they could see there was more media activity, with more antennas peering up over rooflines, and news vans backed up and parked around the corner, even blocking access to the alley. Coming to a stop at the corner, a block from the house, they looked at each other. "We'll never get through all that unnoticed," Amanda said. "What do you want to do?"

"Go home," Risë insisted. "Come on. They can't force us to talk to them." She linked her arm in Amanda's. "If anyone puts a finger on me I'm going to shout blue murder."

"You're not," Amanda argued. "How would it look?"

"Watch me and find out. I have to get home. They're not going to stop me."

They had stepped out into the cross walk when a dark SUV pulled up to block their path. Before either of them could process the situation and panic or holler for help or pull out a phone and dial 911, a tinted window was rolled down, and an identification wallet was held out the window. "Miss Mackie?"

Risë wouldn't budge, so Amanda took a step closer. "Mr. Pope. Do you know what's going on in front of our house?"

"Yes. Get in and we will take you to a hotel."

"No." Risë still hadn't moved toward the car. "I'm going home. I don't care about them. I'm going home." She took a step beyond the SUV just as the light changed and people began to honk.

"Risë, watch out!" Amanda turned back to the car. "Thank you for keeping us updated." She ran forward, grabbed Risë's arm and darted between cars to get them both out of the middle of the street. "Still want to go home?"

Risë shuddered. "More than ever. Who were those people?"

"Well, the one who shoved his identification out the window was one of the men from the State Department who came to see me last month. Remember, I told you about them."

"Oh, Amanda, let's go home. I don't care if we have to throw bricks at people to get inside, I want to go home."

By the time they had reached their street, they had decided to cross over as if they were going to the next block, and then turn and walk along the barricade of illegally parked news vans that would hide their approach and then attempt to blend in to the crowds milling around their front stoop. The plan worked well enough until they took that first step up to the front door. Then flood lamps came on, people started shouting questions, cameras whirred as dozens of images were recorded of them, heads down, scrambling up the steps, trying to avoid microphones and reporters getting in front of them. One man actually put a hand on Amanda to prevent her opening the door, but she turned her cool blue eyes and 'steady' expression on him and pointed out that what he was doing was assault, and she knew a whole bunch of lawyers. He let go pretty quick.

By the time they reached their apartment, Risë was trembling so much she couldn't insert her key in the lock. Amanda took the key from her and opened the door, shoving Risë inside ahead of her in case someone decided to breach the front door and follow them.

"I can't," Risë sobbed, stumbling around the foyer. "I can't do this anymore."

"Yes, you can," Amanda said firmly, dropping her briefcase and coat on the sofa. "You can and you will. Make Gere proud of you, proud of how well you're handling this."

"I'm not handling it. I'm a wreck. A complete, irrational wreck."

"Fine." Amanda tugged Risë's coat off and added it to the pile. "Go sit down and be an irrational wreck. I'll put a kettle on."

"Oh, there you go," Risë sniffed.

"Yes, you're the irrational wreck, I'm the steady one with the kettle." Amanda pointed at a dining room chair. "Sit. I'll be a minute."

A few minutes later she returned to the dining room with a tray. Risë had wept, composed herself and dried her eyes, though they were still red and swollen. She sat up very straight as Amanda appeared, and reached out to help distribute cups and saucers and teaspoons. "I've been horrible," she said, handing a cup to Amanda.

"No, not horrible. Understandably anxious is as far as I would go," Amanda countered.

"No, horrible. Pretty horrible." She passed her cup to Amanda. "You don't know what I've done."

Amanda filled the cup and handed it back, then drew out a chair for herself. "What have you done?"

"It's that photograph. You remember the one I showed you?"

"You showed me several, and all of them were pretty hard to forget."

"Exactly. I keep thinking what if Gere died and we never knew anything more about that girl, about that baby."

"That would be very sad," Amanda conceded.

"Well, I've been looking for some...I don't know what you'd call it...proof of who they are, where they are. I wanted to know more about them."

"Risë, it was none of your business."

"Of course it's my business. I'm his sister. I have a right to know if there's some baby out there who should be calling me Auntie Risë."

"Yes, it would be good for everyone to know, but that doesn't give you the right to invade your brother's privacy."

"Why not?"

"Because. Because it's his business."

"It's mine, too."

"Risë, you *are* being irrational." Amanda put her cup down, untouched. "Now you know how organized and careful your brother is. I'm sure he's made some kind of arrangements in the even that he…that he…" she stopped, not because she couldn't say the words but because their door was swinging open and Mr. Pope and Mr. Peterson were standing there, with their credentials in hand.

Chapter 3

"Miss Mackie?" Mr. Peterson said.

"Yes," Risë said, rubbing her eyes. "Who are you?"

"I believe Miss Kraft can identify us." He continued to hold out his identification, however.

Amanda stood and moved around the table, as if to shield Risë. "What do you want? We don't know any more than we did a month ago – no thanks to you. We can't possibly answer any more questions."

"Are you aware that a grave with two bodies was discovered just outside-"

"Two?" Amanda's heart jumped. "Only two?"

"Then you are aware," Mr. Peterson concluded."

"Only two?" Amanda repeated.

"Only two have been confirmed."

"Have you identified them?"

"That's why we're here." Mr. Peterson turned to nod at Mr. Pope. "We have some photographs-"

Amanda put a hand out to stop Mr. Pope who was opening a portfolio. "Just a minute.

Risë, go wash your face and take some aspirins. Your head must be pounding."

"But, I-"

"Go on," Amanda said firmly, her gaze fixed on Mr. Pope.

"We need Miss Mackie's identification-"

"I can handle the identification," Amanda said, sounding a lot stronger than she felt. There was no way she was going to allow them to subject Risë to photographs of her brother a month after his death.

Risë stood, wobbling. "I can't...I just can't..."

"Risë, go. I'm sure the gentlemen will excuse you."

Risë got as far as the door before she paused. "Amanda, I ought to look. I really ought to."

"No." Amanda went to her, putting her arm around Risë's shoulder. "I don't want those images in your head. Go on, now. I can do this."

She stood in the doorway watching until Risë had gone into her bedroom and shut the door. Then she turned, eyes on fire, to the two Federal agents. "How dare you? How *dare* you? You burst into our lives flinging accusations around about our loved one, then waltz out again without giving us any details at all. Then you think you can come into our home, uninvited, and start subjecting her to pictures of a moldy corpse? What kind of monsters are you?"

Mr. Peterson pursed his lips, as if trying to hold back an outburst of his own. It was Mr. Pope who responded. "We weren't going to show her photos of the corpse. That is not our practice. We have…" he paused to pull a folder from the portfolio, "photographs of effects that were found in the grave with the bodies." He held out the folder. "Do you recognize any of these items?"

Amanda sat down at the dining room table, heavily, and with trembling fingers opened the folder. The effects were just the kind of thing one would expect: a watch, a ring, a religious icon on a chain, a pair of glasses, a decaying lanyard on which could barely be read the word PRESS.

Emotion bubbled up and escaped in a sound that might have been a laugh or a sob. She thumbed through the photographs again. "No," she answered, gasping. "No."

"You're sure? Perhaps if Miss Mackie looked at them, she-"

"No, she'd say the same thing. Gere carries a pocket watch, not a wristwatch. It was his father's. He does not wear a ring, he's not very active in his religion, and even if he were, he's Catholic, not Jewish. His vision is extremely good, and he never, ever wears a press badge. No." She closed the folder. "It's not him." She stood. "Excuse me." She ran down the hall. "Risë, it wasn't him. It's not him!"

Gere's face was back on the television screen that night. Words like 'unconfirmed' and 'unidentified' were tossed around like a dodgeball on the playground, but no one mentioned the State Department, his sister or the fact that the effects in the grave were identified as *not* belonging to Gere Mackie.

The entire ordeal seemed to be Amanda's undoing. She felt too weak to cry, to eat, to sleep, to move. She sat on the sofa the entire night, tissues wadded into her hand, starting at the flickering screen, ignoring Risë's attempts to feed her or begin a conversation.

Risë had wanted all the details of the interview, and then decided she didn't want to know and an hour later decided she had to know. Amanda didn't satisfy her. All she could think about was the joy she had felt when she saw those effects and knew they belonged to someone else; someone else who would be shown those photographs and realize that their loved one was gone forever.

It was only the fact that Gere had considered her 'steady' that enabled her to get up and got into work the next day. And the next day. And the next week. Risë's manic episodes appeared over. They'd had their horrible apex of fear, and now the two women settled into an unhappy but routine existence. They no longer speculated; in fact, they rarely mentioned Gere at all. It was as if they had both accepted, without discussing it with one another, that sooner or later another grave would be found and there would be no doubt about who was in it.

Amanda had stopped watching the news. She would tense up at the opening segment, dreading the inevitable announcement, and when nothing was said, she'd be depressed for hours. It was just easier not to watch.

Risë watched occasionally, but always acted guilty about it when Amanda observed her doing it. She made excuses, claimed to have forgotten it was on, or that it came on after a program she had been watching.

Since both women were avoiding social interaction, there was no reason to talk about, or even think about him. Yet he crept into their thoughts and imaginings all the time. An actor in a movie might tip his head the way Gere did, or a man in the grocery store might laugh as he did, or they might see someone with his hair color walking ahead of them in a crowd. Gere was everywhere, but nowhere.

Even the man climbing out of the taxi near their house as Amanda walked up from the bus stop reminded her of him. The cab had sped past her as she turned the corner, made a U-turn on the one way street, swung up the wrong way on the street, and stopped in front of her building. Two figures had backed out of the cab, throwing bags on the sidewalk. At first she thought her exhausted eyes were playing tricks on her, but then she started to run. "Gere!"

Gere had been paying the driver but, hearing her voice, he whipped around and grabbed her as she reached him, swinging her into the air and holding her as if he never thought to see her again. "Amanda," he cried, bestowing kisses to her brow, her tear filled eyes, her long brown hair. "Amanda, Amanda. Amanda."

She clung to him, more in fear that it was all a hallucination than a desire to be in his arms. He was holding her so tightly his body trembled, and she had the disconcerting idea that he might be struggling with tears.

Behind them, there was a not so discreet cough. Slowly he lowered her to the ground. "Stephen," he said to the other man, "this is one of my girls. Amanda, this is Stephen O'Hara. He was my housemate back when I was living in Kuwait."

Amanda didn't want to let go of Gere, but she managed to extend a hand. She'd never heard of this man, but she was astounded by him. Stephen and Gere could have been twins except that Stephen was perhaps a head taller and his complexion ruddier, but the hair, the eyes, the defined cheekbones, the determined jut of the chin were all the same. After waiting all this time for Gere to come home, they were getting not one, but two. "How do you do?"

"Much better, now," he said, holding her hand up to his lips. "Much, much better."

No, she decided, not so much like Gere, after all. She turned back to Gere just in time to see him scowl. Or perhaps it was just some effect of his absence. He looked thin and tired. His clothes hung loosely on him. His eyes were sunken and tired. His longish hair was flopping around in the breeze as if it were a separate entity. Tears stung her eyes. "Saying that I'm glad to see you back would be a pretty empty statement at this point," she sniffed, easing her hand out of Mr. O'Hara's fingers.

"Not empty at all." Gere scooped up his bags from the sidewalk, and took Amanda's briefcase, as well. "You look done in, honey," he scolded, his eyes going over her face with greedy affection. "I'll bet you got less sleep than I have lately."

"Oh, Gere, you don't know..." Amanda was laughing and crying. "We didn't know...where have you been?"

Something passed over his face, something dark that he didn't want to look at. He glanced away and when he looked back, he had pasted an oversized grin in place. "Come on, come on. I'll tell you both when we're all upstairs." He gestured with the bags. "I don't want to tell the story more than once." He tossed a look over his shoulder. "Bring up the rear, O'Hara, or you'll be left out in the cold. "Is Risë home?"

Amanda could feel something forced and unnatural in his voice but she was too overcome with relief to analyze it. "I expect she is, although I haven't heard from her all day."

"Really? A whole day? I somehow pictured her with her hands glued to the phone waiting to hear the worst." He grinned again.

"Yes, she has her days," Amanda confessed, working her key into the door.

"Well, she's going to hear the worst possible." He pushed her up the stairs. "Her awful brother is home."

At the apartment door, they paused. Amanda was ready to stand back and let him make the grand interest, but Gere gave her a faint shrug and mumbled, "I don't seem to have my key." She pushed her key into the lock and eased the door open. The television murmured from the living room, casting a blue light everywhere. Risë was curled up on the sofa, a hand tucked beneath a pale cheek, her long blond hair spilling around her shoulders. Stephen looked over the back of the sofa and said, "She looks like Sleeping Beauty."

"She does," Gere agreed, and bent over the back of the sofa to brush a tender kiss to her cheek.

Risë's brown eyes fluttered open. Gere smiled at her. She closed her eyes again, shifting on the cushion under her head. Then she opened her eyes again, sat up and threw her arms around him, pulling him off balance and over the back of the sofa like some sort of martial arts trick. "Gere!" she screamed. "Gere! I must be dreaming. If I am, don't wake me up. Gere, oh, Gere, it's so good to see you."

"You're not dreaming, you're awake, and you've permanently deafened me." Gere sat up, unwinding her arms, and rubbing his ear. "Stephen, this is my sister, Risë. Risë, this is Stephen O'Hara. I knew him in Kuwait."

Stephen smiled at Risë. "I can see the family resemblance," he said, and then looked at Amanda, embarrassed. "Isn't she…?"

Gere pulled himself to his feet, dragging Risë up with him. "Amanda's my sister, too…well, sort of." He waved it away. "It's complicated. But, don't I have the prettiest girls in the States?" He kissed Risë's brow. "It's good to be home, Sis." He smiled at Amanda, who stood by, tears streaming freely and his own voice roughened for a moment. "I'll tell you, in all honesty, there was a time when I didn't think I'd ever see you two again."

"What happened, Gere?" Risë demanded, pulling him to sit beside her on the sofa. She left no room for Amanda to join them.

"Do we have any coffee in this place?" Gere asked. "Or have you two been living on it so you could watch me on the news every night."

"Oh, there's plenty of coffee." Risë shot a look at Amanda.

Amanda pretended not to see. She wasn't budging. She wanted to hear what happened to Gere.

"Listen, I've heard this already," Stephen announced. "Show me where the kitchen is, and I'll get some started."

Amanda turned, unwillingly, and indicated the kitchen on the other side of the dining room table. "I'll make the coffee," she offered, trying to be gracious. "Were you…over there, too?"

"I was, technically. I never got off the airfield, though. The local army decided that news people were giving them a bad image in the world, so they wouldn't let us transmit anymore. They were especially angry at your…" he hesitated, rubbed the back of his neck and resumed, "at Gere. There was a bounty on his head. He had to go into hiding. Oh." He stopped and his face reddened. "Maybe I shouldn't have told you that."

"No, that's all right." Amanda glanced back toward the living room. What was he telling his sister that she would only get to hear second hand? Had Risë asked him about the photograph, yet? It hadn't been mentioned in weeks, so perhaps Risë had forgotten about it, or perhaps it was no longer a priority now that Gere was home safe and seemingly sound. "So, I guess you're a close friend of Gere's," she ventured, feeling something was expected of her.

Stephen shrugged, negligently. "Pretty close, I suppose. We shared a house in Kuwait a few years ago. I was on assignment for the BBC." He leaned against a countertop and watched her measure coffee. "So, you're not really his sister?"

Amanda shook her head. "No, I'm just an outrider," she knew she sounded almost bitter, and she tried to soften her tone with a grateful smile, "but, I might as well be a member of the family. Gere's looked after me since my father died when I was in middle school."

"Oh." He glanced toward the living room. "So there's no romance between you?"

Amanda nearly dropped the carafe she was filling with water. "Good Heavens, no!" she spluttered, nonplused. "He's like a brother or uncle to me. Whatever would make you ask such a thing?"

Stephen smiled and took a step toward the sink. "I just wanted to – oh, hello, Gere." His face reddened more deeply and he moved back.

Gere was smiling but it wasn't in his voice. "You just don't quit, do you?" He looked toward Amanda in such an odd way that she wondered how much of the conversation he had heard and did he think she was ungrateful for his kindness? "Amanda, leave the coffee. Risë's driving me crazy to hear what's been going on. I don't want to have to retell the story for you."

She knew he really didn't mean to sound as if sharing this horrible episode in his life with her was a burden he resented carrying, but in the wake of Stephen's questions and the way Risë had cut her out of the homecoming moment, his irritation was another painful reminder that she just didn't belong. She had never felt so out of place as she did at that moment.

"No, that's all right." Her voice fit tight in her throat. "The coffee's practically done, and anyway, Mr. O'Hara has been telling me some of it. I don't know if I want to know details." She raised her eyes from the coffee pot and forced a smile. "Besides, I'm sure you want to be alone with your sister." She switched the power on, and turned, holding herself in check so she did not run as she left the kitchen for her bedroom. "Excuse me."

She must have slept, for the next thing she knew, there was a light tapping somewhere nearby. She lifted her head from the pillow of her arms and sent her eyes around the darkness of her room. A moment later, her door pushed open and Gere's silhouette filled the sliver of light from the hall. "Awake, AJ?"

She sat up, brushing her hair back from her face. He hadn't called her that in years, and it made her ache a little. "Yes, of course. What do you need?" According to the LED readout on her alarm clock it was after ten.

He pushed the door open a little more. "We ordered pizza. Do you want some?"

"No, thank you." She swung her legs to the side of the bed, sitting up and rubbing her eyes.

"Is everything…all right now?" Gere pushed the door open enough to come in and then shut it behind him. He hadn't come into her room in years, either.

"Oh, yes, it's fine." She combed her fingers through her hair. "I suppose I finally let go of all…" Her fingers clenched in her hair and she forced them open as she forced out an explanation for her overdramatic reaction. "This has been very stressful, the not knowing…well," she laughed self-consciously, "I suppose what we went through was nothing compared to your experience."

"Oh, I was fine," he said. They both knew that they were both minimizing the events of the last several weeks. "I just missed you girls and…and pizza."

She reached for her pillow and fluffed it, as if preparing to return to it. "Well, go on and enjoy it."

"Actually…" he looked at her alarm clock, "I think I'm going to get some people out of bed. No one knows I'm back in the States. I'd better let people know I wasn't shot or anything."

"Oh, I'm sure the wheels of the State Department have been turning since before you touched down on American soil," Amanda said dryly. "Although, I'm mystified how you managed to get here without CNN meeting you at the door."

He shook his head, looked over his shoulder and lowered his voice. "I didn't exactly go through official channels. My passport was…I lost my passport so I borrowed one, and –"

Amanda put her hands to her ears. "I can't hear this. I'm an officer of the court."

Gere groped in the darkness, found her bed and sat down beside her. "I'm sorry I put you through all this. I know it was rough – a lot rougher for you than for Risë. You're the one who shouldered all the responsibility." He put a comforting arm around her. "Are you going to be all right?"

Amanda nodded. There was something unnatural about him sitting there beside her – and not just her recently acquired information about his child. He seemed tense and made even more so by his obvious efforts to appear relaxed. "Oh, don't you worry about me, I'm steady as Gibraltar."

"I know," he said with a grim chuckle. "You've always been stronger than Risë, that's for sure." He gave her a little squeeze. "You smell good. I'll tell you, honey, there were times when the only thing that kept me sane was the memory of the way the bathroom smells when you and Risë finish getting ready for the day. So clean. So normal." He sighed and rested his chin on her shoulder. "I guess it was a little rough for me, too."

This was a new person, a different person than her funny, hard-working, dedicated big brother figure. This was a war weary warrior of truth, a tense and tired man reaching out for comfort, a sexual being who had known love and a broken heart, sitting on her bed and reaching out for comfort.

Amanda experienced an unexpected, perhaps inappropriate and faintly familiar ache in her stomach. It reminded her of her first crush, in high school. She had been standing at the piano in the rehearsal hall of the Drama Department, watching Kyle Winslow play some old Paul McCartney tune, and when he looked at her, there as a moment of intense silence, where she felt as if forces beyond her control were willing her to fall into his arms and let him kiss her. But, the choir director came in before she could fall, and the moment passed.

This time it was Risë, pushing the door open and cooing, "Gere, are you coming back out? Stephen wants to show us some of his photographs."

Photographs. That ended the moment more effectively that Risë's inopportune arrival. Amanda stood, brushing her skirt and her hair into place. "What kind of photographs?" she asked, trying to sound very enthusiastic.

"From Eastern Europe. You know, where the Berlin wall used to be, things like that." Risë pushed the door wide enough for Amanda and Gere to file past her, and she gave each of them a curious, probing look.

Even though Gere had brought back discs of just such subjects, Amanda made herself say brightly, "Oh, I'd like to see those." She stopped at the bathroom door. "I've got to wash my face," she murmured. What she wanted to do was splash cool water on her face until the fire was extinguished.

Risë pushed that door open, too. For a horrible, guilty moment, Amanda thought Risë was going to accuse her of something. But, she reached out and squeezed Amanda's arm. "It's so good to have him home," she whispered.

Amanda nodded. She wondered if Risë had sensed something out of character in him, too, or if it was just her overworked imagination.

Risë didn't give her a chance to ask. "What do you think of Stephen O'Hara?"

"I don't think anything, yet." Amanda rinsed her face and patted it dry with one of Gere's spruce green towels. "I've only spent about fifteen minutes with him." *During which he tried to come on to me.* "Honestly, I can't really think of anything right now, except that Gere is home and safe." Of course, after all these years, she knew that Risë had erased the doubt and fear of the last several weeks the moment she opened her eyes and saw Gere smiling at her. There would be no residual trauma or exhaustion for her. She was ready to move on to new interests. "He thinks you look like Sleeping Beauty."

"Really?" Risë got a becoming pink in her cheeks. "Sleeping Beauty? That's kind of cute. Corny, but cute."

"Kind of," Amanda agreed.

Risë reached for Amanda's arm again. "I haven't said anything about those pictures, yet. Have you?"

Amanda put the towel back on the rack. "No, and I'm not going to," she answered primly. "As far as I'm concerned, they do not exist. We never saw them."

"How can you think about that sweet baby's little face and say you never saw them?" Risë argued, her voice rising to a squeak.

Amanda looked down at her, sternly. "I never saw them."

The pink faded, and a darkness came over her face, a darkness of thwarted stubbornness. She sighed sharply. "Come on. Stephen's going to show us his photos." Risë turned and went down the hall, Amanda trailing after her, casting an unwilling glance toward Gere's bedroom door.

Stephen and Gere were sitting on the floor in the living room, beer bottles in hand, looking at Stephen's laptop, as a slideshow of photographs played across the screen. "Girls," Gere announced, without emotion, "Stephen's going to stay with us a couple of days. Is that all right?"

"Sure," Risë said brightly. "That's fine." She gathered the tiered skirt of her cotton dress, and floated to the floor beside Stephen.

"Wonderful," Amanda said. Since she was still in her grey suit and tights, she perched daintily on the edge of the sofa.

"I've got an idea," Stephen announced, smiling at Amanda. "Let's go out tomorrow night. My treat."

Amanda looked at Gere. Surely, after what he'd just endured he wouldn't be up to a night on the town. "Don't you think you need a day or two to get back in sync with this time zone?" she suggested.

"Ah, no," Stephen protested. "I've never seen San Francisco, beyond the airport, and I'm willing to pay for the expert services of three natives to show me around."

"That's a terrific idea," Risë enthused. "We can start with drinks at the Four Seasons, then supper at the Top of the Mark and then dancing at the Verdi Club," Risë ticked off the itinerary on her fingertips. "Oh, and maybe a midnight Red and White cruise." She beamed. "Doesn't that sound great?"

"It's sounds as if we'll be running all over the City," Amanda answered.

Gere was frowning at nothing in particular, but he focused on his sister at her suggestion. "Just a minute, young lady. Who's been taking you on midnight Red and Whites?"

"Oh, put that act back in the trunk," Risë laughed. "I haven't had a curfew in years." She shifted her smile to Stephen.

"That's a point," Stephen pointed out. "We'd better get it straight who's with whom." He looked at Amanda and then back to Risë. "I guess you'll have to be my partner, Risë," he decided. "It would look funny if you were going out with your brother."

Gere met Amanda's uncomfortable expression with a little frown of his own. "Oh, I don't think we need to go to the bother of pairing off," he complained. "It's not as if we're going on a date."

"Oh, but it is," Stephen protested. "Come on, mate, I haven't been on a date in a year. Well, not a proper one, anyway." He reached out and took Risë's hand to press a kiss to it. "Then it's a date, is it? Should I rent something formal for the occasion?"

"Oh, yes, let's all dress up," Risë said, jumping up. "I've got a new dress I've been dying to wear. It's red," she said meaningfully, and then broke into a girlish giggle. "It's outrageous."

"Risë," Gere began.

"Oh, it's not that outrageous." Risë pretended to pout. "Gere's so old fashioned when it comes to us." She flicked a hand to include Amanda. "Then he's archaic."

Amanda couldn't believe her ears. After nearly two months of hell, not knowing if Gere was alive or dead, Risë was ready to party only a few hours after he walked through the door. Couldn't she see how tired he was? Couldn't she feel the pain? Didn't she have any compassion? Didn't she have any sense? She lowered her eyes, embarrassed. Did she have any right to judge how Risë reacted to Gere's homecoming? No.

"It's just that I don't want my girls getting into trouble." He emptied his beer in a gulp. "But, I suppose if they're going out with us they'll be safe enough, won't they, Stephen?"

Amanda looked up from her nervously knotted fingers. Did she hear a veiled warning in that voice? Stephen did seem to be a bit on the prowl, flirting first with her and then with Risë and blatantly one in front of the other.

Stephen seemed to recognize it as a threat, as well. "Absolutely," he said, emptying his own bottle.

"Another, Stephen?" Gere asked. Somehow it didn't seem like an offer, it actually sounded more like a suggestion to stop drinking.

"Not for me," Stephen answered dutifully.

"Amanda, you've worked all week." Gere touched her shoulder as he passed. "Are you up to a big evening out?"

"Oh, please say yes," Risë implored. "If you back out, they won't go. Please, Amanda?

I'll even get up and fix breakfast so you can sleep in tomorrow."

Amanda sighed and looked up at Gere with a helpless 'do I have a choice?' "Of course," she lied, "I'm looking forward to it."

Stephen raised his empty bottle in salute. "So am I," he said with meaning.

Gere glanced at the clock on the mantle. "I'd better go make those phone calls," he said reluctantly. "I'm sure I'll be ordered to some Federal office or another for a debriefing tomorrow."

Amanda's eyes widened in surprise. "Federal-"

"You girls better get to bed." He cut her off, reached down, caught his sister's hand and pulled her to her feet. "See you in the morning, Sis."

Risë gave her brother a tight hug. "I'm so glad you're safe, Gere."

Amanda stood, too. "So am I, Gere."

She was surprised that Gere pulled her into the embrace with his free hand. They hadn't shared a hug like this in years. She hadn't realized how much she missed them and once again the uncharacteristic emotion welled up and overflowed. Amanda burst into tears, broke away and ran back to her bedroom. She was as relieved as Risë that Gere was safely home, but something had changed in his

absence and she didn't think they could ever go
back to the way things were.

Chapter 4

Risë knocked on Amanda's door and stepped inside, giggling, a bathrobe wrapped tightly around her. "Is that what you're wearing?" she said, the giggle fading into a frown of disapproval and disbelief.

Amanda looked in the full length mirror of her closet door. The dress she had chosen was a very demure black crepe chemise with a boat neckline, three quarter sleeves and a skirt that stopped a modest two inches above the knee. "I wore this to the Christmas party at the firm last year," she said, draping a strand of pearls around her neck. Gere had given them both pearls for their eighteenth birthdays and it seemed like a good talisman to wear for the occasion. "Everyone seemed to like it." She turned toward her dressing table.

"I can see why," Risë chuckled.

The back of that demure little dress dipped almost to her waistline and drew attention to itself with a sequined bow of white. Amanda smiled over her shoulder. "Do you approve?"

"Yes." Risë threw her robe open. "Do you?" Risë's dress *was* red. It was lace, short, form fitting, off the shoulder, with a naughty little wisp of lace that ran up one bare shoulder, wrapped around her throat and darted down the other. She did not wear pearls.

"Wow," Amanda said. "That *is* a dress. Gere's going have apoplexy. Is he home, yet?"

"No." Risë paused before Amanda's mirror to check her hair. "He was gone when I got up this morning and I got one cryptic text saying he was still up on 7th Street…whatever that means."

"The Federal Building," Amanda supplied. *Why should a reporter need to be debriefed by the Federal government? There is far more to this story than Gere simply hiding out because there was a bounty on his head.*

Risë seemed to miss the implications. "I wish he would hurry. Stephen will be back soon." She tied the sash of her robe tightly. "I'm going to wear my black velvet cape. Gere won't even know what I'm wearing until we get to the Four Seasons. Oh! There's the door. Gere must be back." She darted out of the room.

Amanda sat down on the side of her bed and slipped into her black velvet mules. Another ill-fitting piece to the puzzle was the complete lack of media coverage in the last day. After the display they had witnessed on their doorstep a few weeks prior, it was astounding that there hadn't even been a swarm of media surrounding his safe return – a Breaking News alert on CNN, at the least.

There was another knock on the door, but it was too firm to be Risë's so it must be Gere. "Come in."

It wasn't Risë and it wasn't Gere. It was Stephen. He looked very nice in a white dinner jacket and black tie. He held his arms out, to show off and get approval, and when he'd gotten that in the form of a smile and nod, he stepped in and shut her door. "I hope you're not upset that I'll be escorting Risë tonight. I couldn't imagine Gere dancing with his sister, could you? And speaking of dances, will you save one for me?"

Amanda looked up at him, thoughtfully. "Wouldn't it be easier just to flip a coin?" she asked, slipping into her other shoe.

Stephen had wounded innocence all over his face. "What do you mean?"

"I mean, I think you think you're going to get somewhere with one of Gere's girls." She stood and moved past him to her closet. "You just can't figure out which one of us the sure bet." She pulled the door open and rummaged around for the box which held her mother's white fox jacket.

"You've got me all wrong, Amanda," Stephen said, behind her, sliding a fingertip down her bared spine.

Amanda reached back to catch his hand and removed it. "No," she said, firmly, "I don't. I'll tell you what I think. I think you're not going to get anywhere trying those tactics on either of us. I see right through you, so they won't work on me. And, even if Risë's intrigued by your 'aw, shucks' charm, she's a nice, old fashioned girl, and she won't succumb, either. And furthermore," she added, pushing past him again, to collect her black velvet evening bag. "If, by some miraculous chance, you did succeed in seducing one of us, Gere would have you killed – in a very, very nasty way." She smiled sweetly as she moved things from her sensible brown leather purse to the evening bag.

Stephen did not react with anger or shame. He smiled at her. "You make that sound like a challenge, Amanda."

Amanda's smile froze and shattered. "It isn't," she promised him.

Risë pushed the door open. "Gere just called. Are you ready to – oh, hello, Stephen." She smiled and tugged her cape close around her throat. "You look very nice."

Stephen struck a pose. "I do, rather."

"Well, it should be a very interesting night, don't you think?"Risë's eyes were twinkling.

Stephen turned and smiled at Amanda. "We'll see," he told her.

Amanda thought about Risë's dress and shuddered. *A nice, old fashioned girl!*

Gere was in black. Amanda was reminded of how much she liked to see him in a tuxedo. He had two gold boxes in his hand, and when Risë, Stephen and Amanda made a parade down the hall, he held the boxes out, giving one to Risë and one to Amanda. "I thought if we were going to make an evening out of this, we might as well do it right."

"Just like Prom Night," Risë giggled, opening the box he gave her. "Oh, orchids." She pressed a kiss to her brother's cheek. "You are an old fashioned sweetheart."

"Thank you, Gere," Amanda murmured.

Gere gave her an expectant stare. "Come on. Don't I get a kiss from *you*, too?"

Blushing, Amanda stood on tiptoe to kiss his cheek.

"Wait a minute!" Stephen cried, dashing into Gere's room. "This night must be immortalized in pixels. Go ahead." He held up his camera. "Kiss him again."

Amanda reached up to obey and, to her surprise, Gere turned, taking her in his arms, and kissed her mouth. Amanda's eyes were wide open and startled as the flash went off.

"Do you want a picture of me kissing him, too?" Risë asked.

"No, I'd rather have one of you kissing me," Stephen grinned, handing the camera to Gere. "Would you mind, old man?"

Gere set his jaw and lifted the camera. Stephen threw Risë back in a classic dip and planted a thorough kiss on her mouth. Gere took the picture and thrust the camera back in Stephen's direction. He looked furious.

"You asked for it," Amanda told him, quietly.

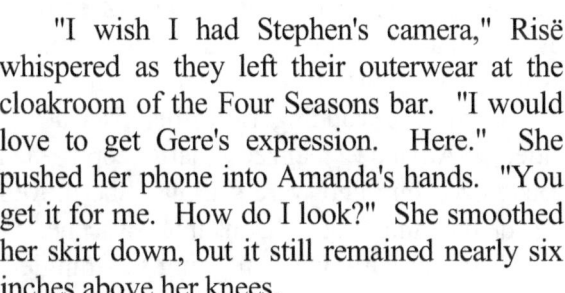

"I wish I had Stephen's camera," Risë whispered as they left their outerwear at the cloakroom of the Four Seasons bar. "I would love to get Gere's expression. Here." She pushed her phone into Amanda's hands. "You get it for me. How do I look?" She smoothed her skirt down, but it still remained nearly six inches above her knees.

Amanda wondered if, as a sister, she would have the right to criticize Risë's appearance, or at the very least, warn her about Stephen's intentions. Since she was not Risë's sister, she elected to do nothing but smile and shrug. "You're going to kill at least one man tonight," she promised. *Or get one killed.*

"Oh, good." Risë giggled as she had been doing all evening, and hugged Amanda's arm. "Here we go."

They stepped out of the cloak room to find the two men engaged in a heated discussion just outside the bar. Stephen, who was facing them, looked over Gere's shoulder, stared and broke into a grin.

Gere glanced over his shoulder, and then jerked around. "Risë," he said, warningly.

Risë smiled and did a little turn. "Do you like it?"

"No," Gere answered bluntly.

"I do." Stephen stepped up and offered his arm. "Shall we?" He tossed a smug smile at Amanda as he passed.

Gere was standing rigid, his fists at his side. Amanda realized that people had recognized him and were staring. She moved beside him and hissed, "Don't make a scene."

"I'm not sure who I'm going to strangle," he vowed, "but I'm going to strangle one of them."

"Fine," Amanda said with a smile to confuse onlookers, "but strangle them in a place with fewer witnesses."

"At least you look like a lady." Gere dropped his arm around her back, realized he was touching flesh and froze, looking over her shoulder. "From the front," he amended.

The evening progressed just as Risë had planned – but, certainly not as Gere had hoped. She and Stephen made an attractive couple, no doubt, and as the evening went on, it became more and more clear that they had certainly found something in common. The later it got, the less they acknowledged the couple with them. By the time they reached the Verdi Club, they sailed inside without even looking back to see if Gere and Amanda had followed. They were on the dance floor enjoying a seventies cover band before Gere and Amanda got inside.

Gere steered Amanda toward a booth, ordered drinks and tried to get his sister's attention, but she was seeing no one but Stephen O'Hara. He sat in the booth and seethed.

Amanda had never seen him so obviously angry except in front of a camera. It was almost frightening to see the rage without the softer influence of his compassion. "How did the debriefing go?" she asked, hoping to distract him.

Gere answered with a jerky shrug of his shoulder.

"Gere, she's a big girl." Amanda patted his arm. "If she wants to make a fool of herself over this guy, you can't stop her."

He jerked away from her hand. "She's *not* a big girl," he argued. "She's naïve and inexperienced and immature." One finger stabbed the air in the direction of the dance floor. "Look, I know this guy. He's a cannibal and she's exactly his idea of a midnight snack."

"Then why on earth did you bring him home?" Amanda asked.

Gere's face turned to stone. "I owed him something," he answered vaguely.

"Did he help you 'borrow' a passport?" she asked. She could understand his sense of obligation, if that were the case.

"I just owed him something," Gere repeated, snapping. "Besides, I thought you couldn't hear anything about that?"

Amanda sighed. She had been sighing all evening. "Look, I can have a headache or something if you want to cut-"

"It won't work, AJ. She won't come home 'til the cows do, now."

"Gere," Amanda sat back in the booth, "she's twenty five years old."

"And he's thirty five. Ten years might as well be a millennium with those two." Gere sat back, too.

Amanda couldn't deny that. She searched the dance floor. "I don't see them anymore, do you?"

Gere sat forward, scanning the room. "No, I don't." He slid out of the booth. "Wait here."

Amanda sighed again, resting her chin on her upturned palm. *So much for the big evening out.* Well, it was all her fault. If she hadn't thrown down the gauntlet, Stephen wouldn't have tried so hard, so fast. If she had played with him a little herself, maybe Risë would have caught on. Maybe if she-

"They're gone."

Amanda straightened and gaped at Gere. "What do you mean they're gone?"

"I mean they're gone. You've studied the language, you know what 'they're gone' means." Gere tugged out his wallet and tossed money on the table. "Let's go."

"Maybe she's in the Ladies room," Amanda suggested. "Maybe-"

"Maybe they've collected their coats and called a cab." He handed her a folded piece of paper.

"Where did you get this?"

"From the coat room clerk" he said through clenched teeth. "Come on."

Amanda stood because he was tugging her arm. As he guided her through the lounge, she unfolded the note. It was written on the back of a Verdi Club napkin. She read it and looked up at Gere. "They're in love?"

Gere pronounced a word that the FCC would never let him say on the air.

Amanda staggered back in surprise, and nearly stumbled as he continued marching forward. "Well, they might be," she argued, trying to make herself believe it. "He says it was love at first sight."

"I don't believe love enters into this at all." Gere handed a tip to the young man in the red jacket, who signaled for the next available taxi. "If he was in love with her, why was he making a play for you, too?" He frowned down at her. "Oh, I forgot your jacket. Hang on a minute." He turned around and trotted back inside.

Amanda was glad he left. She was blushing guiltily and she didn't want him to notice. Maybe she could deny Stephen's attention. Maybe she could convince him that...how did Stephen word it? She looked at the note again...that their souls had touched the first time they shook hands, and they wanted to spend the rest of eternity together. Did that mean he was going to marry her?

The valet was handing her into the passenger side when Gere came back down the steps, her white fox draped over his arm. He grunted their address and slid in beside her. "When I get my hands on that son of a-"

"Maybe they're going to elope," Amanda suggested.

"He's not the marrying kind," Gere assured her.

"How do you know?"

"I know." His tone of voice was so final Amanda knew better than to press it.

She stared at the note she had folded and refolded a dozen times in as many minutes. The truth was that she didn't believe Risë would ever agree to an elopement and miss out on the chance to have her fairy tale wedding. Gere's conviction regarding Mr. O'Hara's character seemed to seal it in stone. "What are we going to do?" she asked.

"Call the police?"

"And tell them what?" Amanda protested, horrified. "We can't claim she was kidnapped. The police won't start a missing persons search for seventy two hours under these circumstances. What good would it do to drag them into it?"

"It might keep me from killing him," Gere said honestly. "Oh, you're right. Let's just go home. Maybe they're sitting there having a good laugh at our expense."

Amanda settled back in her seat. The idea that they had put together an elaborate ruse to frustrate and anger Gere bothered her more than the possibility that they had eloped.

They pulled up in front of the house. Gere studied the darkened windows. Suddenly, he turned around and patted Amanda's fox wrapped knee. "I'm sorry, AJ. This hasn't been much fun for you."

"It's all right." She pushed the door open, not waiting for him. "I've had worse dates."

He winced. "That hurt." He pushed money through the window to the driver and helped Amanda out of the cab. The house was dark and quiet when Amanda used her key. Gere didn't let it remain so. Pushing past her and flicking on every light he passed, he stormed down the hallway, shouting Risë's name. When he pushed her door open and turned on the light, he staggered back, groaning. "Oh, my God, no."

"What is it?" Amanda cried, rushing up behind him, but keeping her eyes averted. She half expected to find Risë and Stephen in bed together. Instead, she found a room that was a disaster of clothing, make-up and other personal accouterment. She pushed into the room and checked her closet. "Her overnight bag is gone," she told no one in particular.

Gere went into his room. When he returned, he actually looked as if he might cry. "All of O'Hara's things are gone." He looked down at Amanda. "Are you sure we can't call the police?"

"Gere," she touched his shoulder, gently, "he wants to sleep with her, not murder her. She's going to be fine. If she chose to go with him, it was her own decision."

"Oh, AJ." Gere pulled her into his arms, "I should never have been given custody of you two. I was a terrible guardian. It's a miracle neither of you turned into ax murderers."

Amanda put her arms around him, tentatively. His uncharacteristic references to violent acts disturbed her. He had always been very gentle in his conversation, unless speaking on world events. Talk of ax murders and kidnapping had never had a place in their home. *What had happened to him?*

Gere's embrace tightened. His body trembled, his shoulders shook just as they had done the day before, but he didn't make a sound.

Amanda stayed in his arms because she didn't know what else to do. She'd never seen Gere cry before, not even when his father died. He was so tough, so strong, always in control, always taking charge. For once in her life, Risë had taken charge and it was going to destroy him. Finally, she pushed away from him. "I'll put the kettle on," she said.

"Yes, that's a good idea." In the hallway, she couldn't actually see his tears, but she could see him trying to brush them out of existence.

She went to the kitchen, filled the kettle and put it on the stove before going back to her room to get out of that dress. She unrolled her stockings, put her shoes back in their box, and slipped her dressing gown over her backless slip and panties – all sensible, steady things to do.

Gere was at the kitchen table, head in hands, but he looked up and tried to smile when she returned. "Tea," he said.

"I'm sorry?" she said, quizzically, tying the sash of her dressing gown into a tidy bow.

He gestured toward the stove. "You're making tea. Risë always said that showed you were more English than American; you're always making tea in a crisis."

"Risë told me that, too. But as it happens I just prefer tea to coffee," she said defensively. "And I don't think I'm more English than American. I barely remember living there. I was just five when we were all reassigned stateside. I really consider myself a native San Franciscan." She got down mugs and doled out tea bags. Gere was still sitting there with his head in his hands. "You know, she might be in love with him," she said.

"No," Gere shook his head. "That love at first sight stuff is just for books and movies."

"How do you know?" The kettle whistled and she took it off the stove. "Have you ever been in love?"

He sat back in his chair, sighing heavily. "Oh, sure, a couple of times. And Risë's been in love millions of times – or so she thinks."

"Exactly." She brought a cup to him. "So it's easy to believe she might be in love again, isn't it?"

"It's easy to believe she's making a fool of herself over the idea."

"Well. Maybe this time it isn't so foolish."

He steeped his tea. "Of course it is. It's ridiculous. She's known him…what?" he sent a sideways glance toward the clock on the mantel, "twenty eight hours?"

Amanda sat down and stirred her own tea. "But, it's not that simple. Not this time. You know Risë's crazy about you. You hung the moon, as far as she's concerned."

Gere's mouth twisted up in an embarrassed little smile.

"Didn't you notice how much you and Mr. O'Hara look alike?"

"What's that got to do with anything?" he demanded.

"Forgive me for playing psychologist," she said, choosing her words carefully, "but it's been on my mind all night. We've been weeks not knowing if you were alive or dead."

"I know, but-"

"And we've spent those weeks thinking about you. I'm sure Risë's spent most of her waking hours thinking about you. Everything she adored about you was gathered into a big pile in her mind. She was obsessed. Then you walk in the door and bring along with you someone near enough like you to be attractive to her and yet safe for her to feel romantic about. Her feelings for him came pre-installed."

Gere made a face of discomfort. "Are you suggesting she was in love with me?"

"Oh, good Heavens, no," Amanda said quickly. "But she was ready to be in love with someone like you. And there he was."

"He's nothing like me," Gere grumbled.

"Well, superficially," Amanda insisted.

Gere started to argue with her theory. But after a few moments he stopped and sighed again. "Maybe," he conceded grudgingly. "But it isn't real. It won't last."

"Why not? Why can't it last – at least for her?"

"Because love isn't like that. It doesn't hit you like a bolt of lightning, you know. Cupid's arrow is slow. It's gradual." He took a tentative sip and continued. "You're with someone and you like her. She makes you laugh. You have things in common. Maybe you don't even think of her as a potential romance, but you do think of her. In the meantime you date other women, but still, you think of this one particular woman. If you see a good movie, or hear a good band, you catch yourself thinking 'she'd like this'. When you've had a bad day you call her up, because you know she'll listen to you. You never think about a long term relationship. You just figure she's always there and you like it that way. You believe all the nonsense about sparks and thunderbolts and roses and poetry and she just doesn't figure into all that."

He paused and took another sip, sitting quiet for a moment. "And then, you'll wake up one morning and see her and say 'wow, I love her. I can't imagine spending another moment of my life without her.'" He pushed the cup away. "That's love. The other stuff is just lust."

Amanda swallowed, tightly, trying to imagine someone wanting sparks and thunderbolts and roses and poetry with her.

"And you've experienced this phenomenon a couple of times?"

"Yeah."

"So…" she looked around the kitchen, pointedly, "where are they?"

"That's the problem…by the time I say 'Wow, I love her,' she's tired of waiting and has moved on."

Or perhaps her ultra-religious family has taken her away. "I'm sorry."

"It happens." He shrugged. "If it ever happens again, maybe I'll catch on sooner."

Amanda looked into her cup, sadly. "I hope so."

He sent her a thoughtful look. "You've never been in love, either. How can that be?"

"You mean, a nice steady girl like me?" Amanda bit her lip and glanced away.

He ignored the pique she revealed. "I mean a pretty, smart girl like you."

"Oh, I don't know." She tossed her hair, imitating Risë's artless mannerism. "I've never had time, I suppose."

"Don't let time get away from you, Amanda. When I was-" he cut himself off and huffed out a sound of heavy emotion. "These last few weeks, I've done a lot of thinking. I found myself thinking I might be at the end of my life and I'd let so many things wait."

Amanda tried so hard not to show emotion but she couldn't prevent the tears. He had, in essence, admitted to her that he had been taken hostage and could have been killed. Her fingers trembled, wanting to reach out to him.

He didn't see her tears, or her trembling fingers. He didn't even see her. She didn't want to know what he saw, because his face changed. "Maybe that's why I'm so disturbed by Risë taking off with O'Hara. I was forced to realize that I gave away a lot of time I should have spent with her – with both of you and I wanted to make that up to you."

Amanda drew a deep breath to clear away the tears in her voice. "There's time now. It won't be like it was before, but maybe now it will be better."

He dismissed her assertion with silence. "Anyway," he rubbed at his eyes, "what I'm trying to say is don't think you've always got the time to meet someone and fall in love."

"Funny."

"What is?"

Amanda gestured at the table between them. "The one person who totally embraces what you've been saying is the one who isn't here to hear it."

Chapter 5

Amanda spent yet another night sleeping in front of the television. She had started out just sitting with Gere while he cruised through the channels, skipping over anything that had to do with him and his miraculous escape from the war zone. Somewhere around two in the morning, after a very late supper of warmed over pizza, she fell asleep. Somewhere around six in the morning, as the sun was turning fog outside into a shimmering grey, she woke.

Her head was in Gere's lap. He was looking down at her thoughtfully, sadly.

"Good morning," she murmured, starting to sit up.

"It's all right, stay there." He put a hand on her shoulder. "You know, I can remember spending nights like this with both of you asleep like this. We stayed up one night to watch Gone With the Wind. You made it to the Reconstruction. Risë was asleep before the burning of Atlanta." He sighed. "That was a long time ago."

Amanda sat up. "You were very good to both of us," she said. Gere was looking at her so strangely. She looked down and saw that her dressing gown had slipped open. She pulled it shut and tried to smile. "Better to me than Risë, really, since I wasn't any relation to you. You didn't have to look after me."

"Of course I did. Do you think I could have handed you over to the foster care system?" Gere stood up and stretched thoroughly. "After the way your mother looked after Risë when she was little, it was the least I could do." He frowned. "I didn't mean it like that. What I meant was that your mother demonstrated what kindness and generosity looked like, and…oh, I'm making a muddle of this." He dragged his hands through his hair. "I don't know if you understood this at the time, but they were going to put you into a juvenile facility until they could find a foster home for you. I couldn't let them do that." He picked up the pizza box and went into the kitchen.

Amanda stayed where he left her, stunned by his revelation, trying to remember what she knew about that time. She had been taken from school by a distant relation of her father's and she recalled much weeping and vowing that blood was thicker than water, but sometime around the funeral that had changed. She had a vague recollection of an attorney coming to visit her while she was staying with the aunt or cousin or cousin's aunt or whoever the woman was. She remembered looking at some papers which addressed her father's will and then there had been an unpleasant conversation between the attorney and the relative…something about not being allowed to be declared her guardian and taken over the management of her financial future. Shortly after that she was told to leave.

She never knew what transpired between her relative's rather cold dismissal and the warm welcome she received at the Mackie house, but now she could guess.

As she reviewed these events, she heard Gere's new phone chirp. A moment later she heard a strangled sob and a thud. She got up and ran to the kitchen. Gere was sagging against the wall, his phone in hand. "They did it," he said, handing his phone to her. "They eloped."

Amanda read the text, just to make sure she had heard correctly. "Oh, thank God," she whispered.

"Are you serious?" Gere demanded. "You thank God for *that*?" He snatched the phone from her hand and began to respond to the text, but he was clearly too distraught to manage the touch screen keyboard, and put it down on the counter with a groan.

"Yes," Amanda answered. "He didn't just seduce her. He didn't drag her off to some sordid hotel. He doesn't consider her just a one night stand, or a challenge or game. He married her. Gere, she must mean *something* to him."

"I want to see a marriage license."

"Believe me, there will be one," Amanda promised, picking up his phone to read the response he'd begun. She hit DISCARD. "Risë would never be a party to tricking you – not even for love."

"Thanks, AJ." Gere straightened and kissed her brow. "You've very good to have around. So sensible. You always have been. Why don't you go get dressed and we'll get out of here, find brunch somewhere. What do you say?"

Amanda nodded, looking at the phone in her hands. If Risë was married, where did that leave her? She looked down at her dressing gown. Where, indeed?

They walked down to Judy's Diner. Gere ordered a huge meal of omelet, French toast, hash brown potatoes and fruit. It was a sure sign that he was upset. Amanda ordered tea and toast, a sure sign that she was nervous. For a long time they talked about innocuous things; the weather, the upcoming baseball season, the view. Finally, while Gere was tossing bits of French toast at the hovering gulls, Amanda screwed up the courage to address something more immediate and pertinent than the Giants' chances at another pennant. "Do you want me to move out?" she blurted.

Gere stopped feeding the birds and looked at her with a puzzled smile. "Where did that come from? Why would I want you to move out?"

Amanda could put together a cogent argument on anything based on the law, but this was beyond the law. This was based on feelings, on obligation, respect, affection and something that she understood but which evaded definition. "With Risë out of the house - and whether the marriage works or not, we both know she'll be moving out - should I be living there anymore?"

Gere continued to smile at her, bewildered. "I don't understand."

"It will be different without Risë there," Amanda explained.

"I don't see why. Look, Amanda," both elbows on the table, he leaned toward her intently, "if I didn't have a sister, and our fathers were gone, and you were going to be turned over to the Juvenile Authorities, I would have done exactly the same thing." He flicked another bit of batter fried bread over the rail. "Maybe I wouldn't have been very successful without having Risë there, but I still would have tried."

"I was a kid, Gere," Amanda agreed. "Not that I'm not grateful for what you did when I was a kid, but I'm not a kid anymore."

He sat back and looked at her, then looked away, and then looked at her again. "Are you saying you think you're in danger living alone with me?"

"No, of course not! But, people might get the wrong idea." Amanda knew she was floundering badly. "After all, you're so famous. It might be bad for your image."

"Don't you worry about my image." He reached out to pat her hand. "Besides, everyone knows you're one of my girls. No one would ever think anything bad about it." He made a decent effort at a smile. "Okay?"

Amanda nodded, but she didn't mean it.

"I don't want you to worry, Amanda. That will be your home as long as you want. Even if I got married. Even if *you* got married. The whole world can get married and that will still be your home." He signaled for the check. "Let's go. Risë and Stephen might be there waiting for us." He pushed the names through his teeth.

They weren't there. There wasn't even a message from them. There were about a dozen messages stuffed through the mail slot from various news agencies wanting interviews, but none of them were interested in the fact that he was in the middle of a domestic crisis and no longer cared what was going on half a world away.

Amanda washed the dishes that had accumulated over the past two days, and started laundry. Gere showered, shaved, started and deleted a dozen text messages to Risë, and paced. They tried making more small talk but they appeared to have run out of things to say to one another. Every time the phone rang or the bell sounded downstairs, they both raced to see who it was. "I wonder where they plan to live," Amanda mused, after yet another news agency called looking for a few exclusive words from Gere.

"Not here," Gere promised, deleting the recorded message with a vicious jab. "O'Hara's not that stupid. Besides, he's based in London. He'll have to go back in a few days." He stopped, gaping. "I guess that means Risë's going back, too."

Amanda made a face. "It's too bad he didn't marry me, then, isn't it?"

He cocked his head in her direction. "No, Amanda, I think I'd hate it even more if he'd done this to you."

That confession surprised her and it showed on her face. "Done 'this'?" she echoed.

"You're a bright, dynamic woman. You're on your way to a brilliant career. Stephen wants someone who wants nothing more than to adore him and keep his house clean. Risë can live with that. She's got no career ambitions. I suppose, based on what I just said, they're ideally suited to one another." He sighed. "No, you would have made a terrible mistake falling for his line, but then, you don't fall for many lines, do you?"

"None," she assured him, knowing exactly what he was asking her.

"Not that you haven't been handed a few, I'm sure." He twirled a finger in the air. "There was that lawyer last year...the one on the embezzlement case. He had a lot going for himself. Seemed charming, good looking, full of confidence. Risë said he had it bad for you." Gere paused, frowning. "I thought he was going to knock you over, but you never even wobbled."

Amanda knew exactly to whom he referred and up close and personal he wasn't that great. She hadn't even been tempted to wobble. "I guess I don't tip easily."

"I never thought Risë would, either. She always seemed to enjoy the hunt too much, liked to dangle and jerk." He stopped frowning and started glaring. "I'd like to-"

"Gere!" Amanda snapped his name like a Marine drill sergeant. "For the last time: they got married."

He stiffened and then slumped against the wall. "You think I'm overreacting, don't you?" he said.

Amanda laughed, grimly. "Your sister stood right there and said the same thing to me less than a week ago. She was talking about you."

He still looked angry but there was an icing of bewilderment, as well. "She thought I should get married?"

"No, she was…" Amanda could confess what Risë had said. "I don't remember what it was about, exactly, but it doesn't matter. You're here alive and in one piece, and she's a willing participant in an elopement. I don't understand why you are so angry."

"You don't know this man as I do," Gere answered.

"I know him well enough to know that he's shallow and careless and full of himself. Regardless, give your sister some credit. She's an educated, albeit sheltered, woman who has always known what she wanted and, for better or worse, he's the man for her."

"All right, I surrender." Gere raked his hair out of his eyes. "So tell me, should we give them a party to celebrate this romance of the century?"

"That might be nice," Amanda said, but doubtfully. She didn't think she could bear to see Stephen's smug face again. "I know Risë would like to know you're going to accept her decision."

"No, Risë would just like an excuse for a party. She would like anything that involved presents and a spotlight shining on her."

"You make her sound spoiled," Amanda scolded.

"She is" he answered baldly. "She's my sister, and I can say it. She's spoiled rotten and I've got no one to blame but myself. I've catered to her every whim, and protected her from every disappointment in my power. How did you turn out so down to earth? I thought I raised you both equally."

"You did. You were very fair, but you must remember we started out two different people." Amanda noticed a glass left on a table near the window and she went to pick it up. "And stop talking about her in the past tense, as if she's dead. I've had enough of that." She headed back to the kitchen.

Gere hung his head, ashamed. "Sorry," he mumbled.

Amanda glanced at him as she passed. He didn't look sorry. He looked...it was that same faraway look she'd seen earlier. And it was frightening. Impulsively, she patted his arm and was surprised when he flinched.

"Sorry," he repeated, drawing breath in through his nose as he straightened. "Anyway, will you help me plan a little wedding party? I wouldn't know who to invite, or what to order or anything."

Amanda rinsed the glass and put it in the dish rack. "You know what parties are like."

"I don't give parties, I just go to them."

"Poor you." She wiped her hands. "When would you like to have this fête?"

"Well, we've got to find out when they'll be available, first. For all I know, they might go right from Reno to-" he cut himself off, marched out of the kitchen, down the hall to his room and returned a moment later. "They'll have to come back here," he said triumphantly, holding up a green folder. "I've got her passport."

Amanda didn't like the way he crowed. She understood that being responsible for raising her made his relationship with Risë was more complicated that the average brother and sister. She understood that there was something in his history with Stephen O'Hara that made the man an unsuitable suitor in his eyes, but this almost maniacal pleasure he took in thwarting the plans of two legally married adults disturbed her and she wanted to end the conversation. "Get me the details, then, and I'll plan a party."

"Thanks, AJ." He left the kitchen, whistling, but Amanda had the feeling it was just for show.

They were eating homemade raviolis and pesto in front of the television that evening when Risë finally called. She was breathless with excitement – Amanda could hear her even though Gere held the phone to his ear. They had flown to Reno, married in a little chapel next to a waterfall, and now they were on their way home. Yes, they had a marriage license. Yes, they were going to stay in a hotel. Yes, they were moving back to London in a few days. Yes, they would love a party. Yes, she was very, very happy.

Gere put the phone down and looked at Amanda, who was eating raviolis and trying to pretend she wasn't paying any attention to the phone call. "I guess you were right," he said, flatly. His tone had been dull as gunmetal since his outburst in the kitchen that morning.

"I'm glad," she said, around a bite of pasta, "for your sake as well as hers."

Gere pushed food around with his fork, distracted. "You're working tomorrow, aren't you?"

Amanda looked up. She hadn't expected a question like that. "Yes, of course."

He shrugged. "I have an appointment on Market in the afternoon. Maybe I'll meet you downtown for lunch. Okay?"

She nodded. "Sure." He'd never done that. She wondered if he even knew how to find her office. "Why?"

He looked at her, irritated. "Do I need a reason?"

She shrugged, slightly. "In view of law, you would, when past practice never included doing that."

"Past practice…are you telling me I've never come to have lunch with you? Ever?" He thought about it, searching his memory for a fact to counter her assertion. Then he surrendered. "They'll be coming by in the morning to get some of her things. I have a feeling I'm going to need someone to talk to after she leaves."

"Gere." Amanda touched his hand. She had been practicing this speech all day. "I think it's normal for a big brother to worry about his little sister when she gets married, no matter who she is, no matter who she marries. You've got it doubly bad since you've raised her since she was so young. But, you've got to be a little bit happy, too. For the first time in your life, you're completely free. You don't have any responsibilities. You can do anything you want because you don't have to worry how it will affect Risë."

"I still have you to think about," he countered.

Amanda shook her head. "I don't count. I'm not really your responsibility. Not anymore. I've got a job. I could get a place of my own, if I had to. If you wanted to pack up and...and move back to Kuwait, you could." She looked up, wondering how he would react to that suggestion.

He did. He made a bitter face. "Please. They couldn't pay me enough to live there again. I like San Francisco. I was born here, and I've made up my mind that I'm going to die here. I also plan on doing a little living here in the middle. As for doing whatever I want, I have been. Haven't you noticed?"

"Well," Amanda stood and took their plates. "I have noticed that you haven't exactly gone out of your way to have a relationship with a woman. A long term one, that is. Maybe now you'll feel free to think about a wife and children of your own." Again she waited for a response.

He made another face, though this one had a touch of amusement to it. "Are you pumping me about my love life, Amanda Jeanne? Because, if you are, let me assure you that I have plenty of female companionship. I've just never felt it was appropriate to bring women home and parade them in front of you and Risë."

"Well, now you can if you want to." Amanda started for the kitchen.

Gere got up and trotted after her. "Wait a minute. Wouldn't you feel uncomfortable if I brought women home to spend the night?"

"No." She rinsed plates. "Would you feel uncomfortable if I brought men home to spend the night?"

"I feel uncomfortable just discussing it in the abstract." He took the plates from her and stacked them in the dishwasher.

"Then I won't do it." Amanda took soap from a cupboard and filled the little reservoirs. "It is your house, after all."

"And yours," he argued.

Amanda shut the dishwasher with a bang and pushed buttons. "Not really."

"Hey." He caught her arm. "What's with you? All day long you've been acting as if you couldn't wait to get out of here. Are that unhappy living with us?"

"Not at all." She looked down on his hand. He didn't seem inclined to move it. "It's just that I've been thinking about this ever since...well...for some time. I'm not really family. I'm over eighteen so your guardianship has ended and you have no legal obligation to me. I'm just here until it occurred to you one of you to tell me to go."

"Amanda." He reached up and brushed her hair back to study her face. "I'm not going to tell you that. Don't you get it? This relationship has nothing to do with legalities or obligations. You're as much a part of this family – a part of me – as Risë is." He touched his chest, in the general area of is heart. "If you had run off with Stephen O'Hara, I would have been just as worried, just as hurt. I've been just as proud of you as I've ever been of Risë. Your victories have always been my victories. Your tragedies have always caused me pain. Don't you get it, honey? I love you." He kissed her cheek. "You're one of my girls."

Amanda blinked away tears. She felt betrayed. For a moment, just a moment, she had let herself believe that there were more than legalities and obligations. For a moment, she thought the feelings he had were born somewhere beside his sense of duty. For a moment, she had thought, she had hoped, when he said he loved her, it wasn't the same way he loved Risë. She realized she didn't want to be just part of the family anymore. She wanted to be recognized on her own merit. She didn't want to be one of his girls. She wanted to be his woman.

Chapter 6

Amanda knew he was coming even before she saw him stride through the glass doors from the lobby to the clerk's desk. She had heard the excited whisperings up and down the hall: 'Gere Mackie, Gere Mackie'. He stopped just in front of the clerks' desk, where three females paused, mid-task, to look him over from black jeans to green sand-washed silk shirt, and sighed in unison. He was smiling, but it stopped at the dimples and never made it to his eyes. "Amanda Kraft?" he inquired politely.

One of the clerks pointed.

Amanda ducked back into her cubicle before he turned, forcing herself to take several deep breaths as she gathered her bag and jacket. No matter how much she wanted to hear the details of his meeting with his sister and new brother-in-law, she was uncomfortable about seeing him. He was different and that made everything else different.

That morning, he had barged into the bathroom while she was applying her make up. He had done it a hundred times over the years, and he had seen her in her shortie gowns before, but, with the two of them alone in the house, it suddenly seemed uncomfortable and awkward. Well, it seemed that way to her. It didn't seem to bother him at all, and that bothered her all the more.

He turned and saw her stepping out of her cubicle, brushing her hair back from her face, trying to look calm and pleased to see him. "Are you ready?" he asked.

"Yes." Shouldering her bag, she preceded him through the glass door. "How did it go?" she asked, feeling a dozen stares follow her as they left the office and knowing she would be interrogated as soon as she returned from lunch.

"Fine." He strode across the lobby and jabbed buttons on the elevator panel.

She knew it had been anything but fine. She knew something had turned his spine to concrete and his face to steel. She knew that he was welling up with fury and, were he any other man, he would have been raging and swearing and breaking things. She knew all of this but, because they had company riding down to ground level, Amanda didn't press; as soon as they stepped out into a glorious early spring day, she stopped and faced him. "Don't lie to me. I know you're lying. How bad was it?"

Gere looked up into the sunshine as if he'd never seen such a phenomenon before. After a moment, he sighed and his shoulders sagged a little. "She looks happy," he said, doubtfully. "He looks smug. She wants to have babies." He lowered his eyes and looked around the concourse. "He wants us to forgive and forget."

The ludicrous expectation hung heavily between them while they avoided one another's eyes. Amanda pointed to an *al fresco* café across the street, but he steered her toward a cab. "I don't feel like sitting under the stares of a thousand people. Let's go somewhere quiet."

He took her to a restaurant several blocks away; a former speakeasy, it had been turned into a private club generations ago, and now was just a dark place with high, private booths and decent sandwiches. Amanda tried to stir up conversation as she eased into the booth. "You haven't been arrested for homicide, so it couldn't have been that bad," she waited for a response, "unless they haven't found the bodies, yet."

Gere finally answered with an irritated sigh. "You should have seen her, AJ. She was like something out of a Doris Day movie. All she could talk about was starting a family - making babies were her words, not mine.

Damn it, she could have gone to medical school, or go into research. She ought to be making something besides babies."

Amanda was surprised by Gere's diatribe. Of course, she had no idea what Gere's feelings were on family, but she thought he must have a little regard for children – for at least one child. "Let her build her family while she's young," she advised. Personally, she had never envisioned Risë as a scientist. She couldn't remember to buy chicken to make chicken and rice. Making babies seemed appropriate for Risë – providing someone else made sure they got fed. "Just because she got married and wants children doesn't mean she won't pursue something later on. Having children might...settle her."

"Thanks, AJ." Gere reached out and squeezed her hand. "You're such a comfort to me, right now." He opened the menu. "They're leaving for DC next Sunday for his debriefing."

"So soon?" Amanda gasped.

"Well," she could see him shrug behind the enormous menu, "that's just for a few days; they're probably going to come back here to say goodbye before they leave for London. Probably." He closed the menu. "I thought Friday night would be a good night for the party."

"That would be fine." It wasn't fine. "I'll start working on it tonight. How many guests?"

He didn't seem inclined to answer. He was frowning in her direction.

She fidgeted with her napkin under the table, feeling as if he was dissecting her, and yet not even seeing her. "Gere? Is something wrong? Would you rather-"

"O'Hara made a pretty snide remark this morning. I almost clocked him."

"What did he say?"

"He said…" his face flushed as dark as the room around them and he shook his head. "Never mind. You don't want to know."

She shook her head, too. "I think I already do."

He brought his fist down on the table with such ferocity that silverware rattled, and other diners looked up, in surprise. "Damn it, I should have-"

"Gere, it's all right, really," she whispered. "Let it go."

"And to think he married my sister. I *am* going to clock him."

She put her hand on his fist. "Forget about it. How many guests should I invite for the party?"

He glowered at her.

"I have to know," she insisted. "Forget about O'Hara and let's focus on making a nice party for your sister."

He muttered something as dark as his expression.

"Gere."

He lifted his eyes to hers, wide in surprise. "My God, Amanda, just now you sounded exactly like your mother. Maybe you're the one who should be getting married and making babies."

Amanda shrugged and broke a piece of world famous San Francisco sourdough bread from the loaf that was left on their table, relieved that they had shifted the direction of the conversation without violence. "One of these days." She nibbled. "What about you? You've certainly got the fatherhood role down pat. Why don't you start raising your own pedigree newshounds?"

Gere looked neither guilty nor full of regret. He just looked bemused. "Someday. I don't know…with all the chaos and turmoil and hate that I see every day, all over the world, I have serious doubts about bringing any more children into the world. And I see so many so called 'perfect' marriages exploding. If I lost someone that meant that much to me, I don't think I could cope. I mean, look how I reacted to Risë moving out."

That he said 'moving out' not 'getting married' was very telling, Amanda thought. "That's because Risë is the only family left and she-"

"Besides you."

Amanda ignored his statement. "And she left so abruptly. You had no chance to acclimate yourself to the idea."

Gere leaned an elbow on the table and smiled. "You should have been a psychologist, not a lawyer. You're really rooting for them to make it, aren't you?"

"I want Risë to be happy." She smiled as the server brought them coffee, and plates of green salad. "I want you to be happy."

Gere picked up his fork. "And what about you? Who's making sure you're happy?"

"Oh, I am happy," she promised, picking up her fork.

He drew a deep breath and let it go forcefully as if clearing out the ashes of his anger. "Well, seeing you has helped me a great deal. You've really cheered me up." He took a bite of mixed greens and chewed, glancing at his watch. "Eat up. I don't want you to be late back from lunch."

Amanda knew she had plenty of time, but he was suddenly shoveling food into his mouth with such purpose that she didn't think he was really concerned about *her* punctuality.

They ate in silence for several minutes, Gere checking his watch now and then. Finally, Amanda sighed and put down her fork. "Gere, if you need to be somewhere, I can get back to the office on my own."

He had the grace to look a little embarrassed before he caught the waiter's eye and gestured for the check. "I do have an appointment. Stay. Take your time." He stood and slid his wallet from his pocket. Here." He pushed a credit card across the table. "Get the lady a cab when she's through, will you?" he instructed the waiter. "Oh, I almost forgot. I won't be home for dinner – for a couple of days. The President's going to be L.A. lobbying for his new spending package. I'm going down to cover it."

"So soon? You just got-"

"Yes, I know but I have to get back on the horse, don't I? Might as well be sooner than later." He tucked the wallet away. "And I was specifically invited. Is that going to be a problem?"

"A problem? No." Amanda thought about it. "It will seem strange having the place all to myself. I don't think that's ever happened before."

Gere shrugged. "It might be fun." He dropped a kiss to the top of her head. "Thanks for lunch."

"You're so welcome," she muttered as he disappeared into the darkness of the restaurant.

It wasn't fun. Amanda, although a very solitary person by nature, had never really been alone before. She tried to focus on housework, but there wasn't much. There was a service which came in once a week to do the deep cleaning, and with Risë out of the house, there was very little clutter. There was no point in cooking for one person and trying to plan for Risë and Stephen's party just made her boil with rage thinking about Stephen's smug face conveying that he had gotten his way, or imagining the insinuating grins he had tossed Gere's way.

Gere called regularly, as he had always done, and it was strange to have him all to herself in a conversation. They really didn't know what to say to each other. He told her about the President. Being fairly liberal in his politics, he didn't care for this President personally or politically. He talked about the early spring heat wave, the smog and being invited to an impromptu party up in the Hollywood Hills, where he was introduced to dozens of celebrities, and everyone confused him with an actor with whom he had a name in common. He didn't understand it, he told her. He'd met the man and they looked nothing alike. But for all of his effusive chatter, he really sounded as if he was struggling to find something to say.

Risë called once. She wanted to talk to Gere, but when she found out he was in Los Angeles (which she would have known just by looking at a television), she was almost eager to talk to Amanda. Yet, they, too, had nothing to say to one another. For the first time in their nearly twenty years of friendship, these two women had nothing to say.

By Thursday night, Amanda was miserable. At the office, she was grilled about her relationship with Gere Mackie. She lied and told everyone he was her stepbrother. At first everyone was doubtful. Then they were indignant that she had not revealed this pertinent evidence before. Then everyone wanted to meet him. Women who had never had any use for her suddenly wanted to be her bosom friend. Men who had never considered her worthy of their attention suddenly wanted to take her out, take her to dinner, take her back to her place.

But the worst of all was coming back to that apartment, so filled with the essence of Gere and Risë, and feeling every day a bit more like an outsider, like an intruder, like a burglar stealing their time.

Thursday evening she was so miserable that she skipped dinner completely and went to bed. She tried to read, but nothing held her interest. She tried to research precedents for an upcoming trial, but she couldn't concentrate. Everything was so wrong now. Everyone had changed but her. Risë had married, moved out, and grown up overnight. Gere, who was usually so easy going, so invested in 'his girls', was distant, and easily angered. Her home, her family, had disappeared and left her sitting in the rubble. She ended up crying herself to sleep.

When Gere got home, after midnight, he must have heard her sniffling into her pillow because he came to her bedroom door and knocked. "AJ?" he called. "Honey, what's the matter?"

Amanda pressed the pillow to her face, and willed him to go away.

Of course, he didn't. He dumped his bags on the floor and pushed her door open. "Amanda, what is it?" He came to the bedside and brushed her hair from her face, discovering the dampness of tears on her cheeks. "What is it?"

She shook her head and twisted away. "Go to bed, Gere," she mumbled. "I don't feel like talking tonight."

"I can't go to sleep with you crying your eyes out just down the hall." He slid his arms under her and lifted her out of the bed. "Come on."

"Will you put me down?" She tried kicking but he merely tightened his grip. "Gere Franklin Mackie, what do you think you're doing?"

"Taking you to bed," he answered, dropping her on the side of his bed. In the mirror over his bureau he saw the disbelief and dread in her expression. "AJ! Nothing like that. I just want to sleep." He jerked the bedclothes back. "Come on, get under the blankets."

She pushed the bedclothes away and sat up. "Gere, I can't sleep with you," she protested, angry that he didn't understand why she thought it was improper, angry that, when he did understand, he had appeared disgusted by the very idea.

"Sure you can." He was shrugging out of a chambray shirt. "You two used to do it all the time – especially after you watched scary movies."

"Yes." Amanda saw herself in the mirror and yanked the duvet from the bed to cover what the sheer lemon colored nightgown did not. "But we were little girls and we were together." *And if he's still thinking of me as a little girl after seeing me like this, there is something seriously wrong with one of us.*

"Amanda." He stopped, his navy trousers half way to the floor. "Are you telling me you don't trust me anymore?"

Oh, look at him standing there, half naked, and the image of wounded indignation! she thought in irritation. *As if I'm the unreasonable one.* "No, I'm just saying that this behavior isn't appropriate for us." It had been years since she had seen him in nothing but his boxers, and the last time she really hadn't been old enough to appreciate the maleness, the beauty of his body.

"I don't know," he said, putting the trousers over the back of his desk chair. "I think it's more appropriate for a thirty five year old man to have a twenty six year old woman in his bed than a nineteen year old boy to have two eleven year old girls.

"It was different then," Amanda protested. Gere had never done anything that should trouble Risë or Amanda. He had been a comforter and protector and nothing else.

He was still considering his previous statement. "I never thought about it when you were younger, you know? But if someone told me today that he'd had two eleven year old girls in his bed, I'd be first in line to knock his block off."

"Gere! It wasn't like that!" Amanda protested. "We all knew that." Gere would never have thought like that before...and he certainly wouldn't have considered violence as a solution.

"Just seems sort of perverted and..." he shuddered, "creepy, now."

She sank down on the side of the bed. "It wasn't like that. We all knew it."

He shook off the disgust. "Well, it's going to be different now." He climbed into the bed. "Come on." He pulled her down beside him and pulled the blankets up to her chin, sighing in satisfaction. "I hate hotel rooms. They're so unnaturally dark and unnaturally quiet and I get so lonely." He was quiet for a moment. "It's not a matter of sex, Amanda, if that's what you're thinking. Not then, not now. I get women hanging all over me - sometimes even men. I had a Presidential aide give me her hotel room key last night."

Amanda was lying rigidly beside him. "Did you use it?"

She felt him chuckle beside her. "I'm not going to tell you. But, you can rest assured that there won't be any subconscious molestation tonight." He reached up and turned off the bedside lamp. "Now, are you going to tell me what's got you so blue? It seems every time I've looked at you since I got back you've been in tears. Is there some guy who's been given you a bad time? Wait a minute." He lifted up on an elbow. "You aren't upset because Stephen chose Risë and not you."

"Oh, my – no!" Amanda sat up, tugging the duvet up with her. She shuddered, rubbing her arms. "But, that's part of it," she confessed at last. "I feel so guilty."

"Guilty for what?" He sat up, too. "Did you encourage him to elope with Risë?"

"No. Not exactly."

He reached over and flicked on the light. "What does 'not exactly mean?"

Amanda looked down at the duvet. "The night they...the night all this happened, Stephen came into my room. He was trying this stupid line on me and I told him I knew what he was up to. He had me backed into a corner and was trying-" she stopped because she could feel anger oozing out of Gere. "I let him know it wasn't going to work," she said hastily. "I told him I was onto to all his tricks and that Risë was a nice, old fashioned girl and she wouldn't fall for it, either. He told me he c-couldn't resist a ch-challenge. Oh, Gere, it's all my fault." She turned against his shoulder and began to cry again.

"Come on, Amanda," he soothed, stroking her hair. "It's not quite that bad. After all, as you're always pointing out, they got married. She seems happy, and even if the worst had happened, you didn't give him any ideas he didn't at claim at Customs when we landed. Now, stop crying. Come on. I can't stand to watch you cry." He lifted her chin to look into her eyes. "I'm not mad at you, Honey. She's not mad at you. I'm sure Stephen's not mad at you. It's okay." He stroked her brow. "Now, stop crying. That's a good girl. It's pretty conceited of you to take credit for what they did. After all, you weren't even there."

She started to protest but was interrupted by one of those little tremblers that was part of living in San Francisco. They happened so often she never paid any attention to them.

But Gere did. His eyes went dark, and his body went rigid, and he fell on her, holding her down, his hand clamped tightly over her mouth.

Amanda felt a jolt of fear race through her. The weight of his body kept her immobilized, she couldn't even struggle as his hand cut off her breath. But it was his expression that frightened her: he looked frightened for a moment, looking over his shoulder to the doorway, as if he expected gunmen to burst in, weapons blazing.

It took nearly a minute for him to relax, sliding his hand away from her face. "Amanda, I..." He pulled back. "Amanda," he breathed, opening his eyes. "Are you all right?" He pulled a hand across his eyes, shaking. "Oh, man, I am so..." He rolled out of bed, groping for his trousers. "I'm going for a walk." He scooped up his shirt and shoes and slammed doors all the way down to the street.

Amanda sat up, touching her bruised mouth. What had just happened? She had never seen Gere react like that. He had appeared absolutely terrified of some monster only he could see, and for that moment, he was in another place and she didn't even exist.

Chapter 7

When she woke up the next morning, her eyes burning, her head pounding, she was still in Gere's bed. She didn't have to struggle with confusion, wondering how she happened to spend the night there. Even if she didn't remember every detail, her mouth still felt tender and a bit swollen, and she could still feel the rigid fear that had overtaken his body as he held her down.

It was so far out of his character that if anyone had ever suggested that Gere would harm her or Risë, Amanda would have been furiously indignant. But Gere had changed since he returned, and consequently everything around him had changed, including her. That which had always been safe, comfortable and sacred was now rubble at her feet; she was walking a new path, and with a stranger.

She sat up and stretched her aching muscles. Sunlight was trying to sneak past the fog and fill the bedroom. It was six thirty. Where was Gere? She wrapped one of his blankets around her shoulders and slipped out into the hall. He wasn't in Risë's room. He wasn't in her room.

Exchanging the blanket for her dressing gown, she went to the kitchen and started water for tea. Then she went into the living room. Gere was asleep on the floor beside the sofa, his feet bare, his shirt unbuttoned, his fingers curled around the television remote. His lips were parted slightly and his breathing seemed ragged. She would have left him there but, backing away, she encountered one of the occasional tables and a ceramic figure from Holland rattled against the wood.

Gere jerked and opened his eyes. He looked at her for a long time, and sat up, dragging the back of his hand across his mouth, running his fingers through his hair, blinking up at her. "Are you okay?" he asked, hoarsely.

Amanda nodded. He didn't look well. His face was flushed, his eyes were cloudy. "Are you?"

He nodded. "Oh, yeah, I'm fine." He looked at the remote control in his hand and put it on the coffee table before pulling himself up. "Amanda, I'm sorry about-"

"Please." She held up a hand. "Please don't. There's no need to discuss it."

"We have to discuss it," Gere argued, but he seemed relieved.

Amanda wanted to change the subject. No, she wanted to pretend that the subject never existed. "You sound sick."

"It's nothing. A little cold, probably." He dropped heavily onto the sofa. "I was bound to get one. After the last few weeks my immune system is probably pretty compromised, and last night I walked up and down the beach in my bare feet." He shrugged and smiled weakly. "Just a matter of time. Is that the teapot? I would love some tea."

"You would have had to walk eight blocks to get to a beach," Amanda said, not moving.

"That's true." He looked toward the kitchen. "Tea?"

Amanda hesitated a moment longer. She didn't want to revisit the topic, but she did want to know what drove him to walk eight blocks to the beach on a cold, foggy night in March. Deciding she might not like the answer, she darted into the kitchen. *What are we going to do?* she wondered, as she prepared a cup of herbal tea for him.

"Make it extra sweet, will you?" Gere stumbled into the kitchen and settled at the table. "My taste buds seem to be sick, too."

"We'll have to cancel the party," Amanda decided, putting an additional spoonful of sugar in his cup.

He laughed roughly and coughed again. "We wouldn't dare. Risë would want that party even if it was a combination wedding party and wake."

"Don't!" Amanda felt herself cracking, felt rage and fear and disappointment pushing to escape the tight confines of her feelings. "D-don't say that. We thought...for so long we thought..." She shook her head and put his cup down before him with a clatter. "Just don't."

"I'm sorry. You're right. That was thoughtless of me." He pulled the cup closer and leaned over it, letting the steam bathe his flushed face. "I'll be all right. I'll take some aspirins and an antihistamine and I'll be just fine."

Amanda brought her own cup to the table and looked down at him. "Do you want me to move?"

Slowly, he raised his eyes. He looked stunned...no, he looked hurt. "Why do you keep asking that? Do you want to move out?" He pushed the cup away and pressed a hand to his chest. "Of course I don't want you to move, but if you aren't going to feel safe around me – Amanda, I swear I don't know what happened last night. I guess I was afraid of losing you, too." He reached for her hands and held them tight. "You know I would never hurt you. You're one of my girls. It would be like asking me to hurt myself. I couldn't do it. Please, please, Amanda, don't hate me for what happened last night."

Amanda eased her hands away, feeling heat rising to her cheeks. "I don't hate you. Don't be so dramatic." She tried to laugh. "I think we're making more out of this than is necessary." But were they? Amanda knew just enough about Post Traumatic Stress Disorder to wonder if Gere was affected. She wondered if she should suggest that he see someone.

"I nearly broke your neck," Gere said deliberately, "and it was a miracle that I stopped. Now," he reached out to turn her back to face him, "do you want to move out?"

"You didn't – I mean, it wasn't deliberate, Gere. And…"

"And?"

Amanda considered her options. She decided to be honest with him – within limits. "Gere, do you think it is…possible that you might be suffering from some kind of…you know, emotional trauma? I am no expert but since you've been home you've been…not yourself." She rushed on as he tried to protest. "And as for me, we both know I can only stay here as long as you tolerate my presence. I don't have anywhere to go right now, but I suppose I can rally the resources if I had to."

"You're saying you don't feel safe with me, that I've become some kind of lunatic," he accused.

"I did not say that," she protested. "But, Gere, something's not right. I don't know what happened to you while you were gone, but you're so angry and jumpy that I can't help wondering if you were tortured or-"

He slapped her.

Not hard. Not even enough to sting. Just enough to stem the flow of words.

He looked at her.

She looked at him.

He lowered his eyes. "I'm sorry," he breathed. "I'm...I've never...I'm sorry."

Amanda didn't even realize she had cowered. She straightened and avoided his eyes. "Forget it. I was talking too much."

He said that word again. "You weren't out of line. I was. I know your dad believed in hitting. I didn't. I swore I never would, and I never did when you were a kid. I don't think it's any more acceptable now that you're an adult." He looked at his hand as if just realizing it was his. "I'm sorry. That was so incredibly uncalled for. Maybe I'm the one who should move out." His voice dropped to a whisper. "I don't think I'm totally in control of myself right now." He drew a deep, raspy breath and began a speech. "For the record, Amanda Jeanne Kraft, I do not want you to move out. You're part of my family. In fact, you *are* my family. I don't know how many times, in how many ways I can tell you that. I know that I did what I did last night was horrible and inexcusable and I can't even tell you why I did it but it wasn't your fault. I'm not sure what's going on in here..." He pressed a finger to his temple. "Anyway, you aren't going to be my downfall. Unless you leave me."

Amanda touched her cheek. She hadn't even thought of her father when Gere slapped her. She only wondered what had happened to Gere that he would do something so out of character. What had he endured over there? She couldn't leave him alone now. Someone had to look out for him. "All right," she said quietly. "I won't ask again, if you won't apologize for last night again."

"Fair enough." He coughed again.

Amanda looked around the kitchen searching for another subject. She saw the calendar with the big red circle around the day. "Were you planning to bring a date?"

He looked up again and she could see him repeating the question in his head. "I hadn't thought about it," he said after some deliberation. "Will you?"

She nodded.

He looked over his shoulder at the calendar. "Were you planning to…before?"

"No."

"Neither was I. Do you suppose we've left it a little late?"

"No, I don't think so." She fought an urge to touch her cheek again. It didn't hurt, just felt unreal. "You won't have any trouble getting a date because you're Gere Mackie. I won't because I know you and you're Gere Mackie. Everyone wants to meet you. I've become a celebrity now that people know I know you."

He made a face. "I'm not a celebrity. I'm a journalist."

"You're a journalist who made news," she pointed out.

Gere shrugged. "Not intentionally."

Amanda looked at the kitchen clock. It was nearly seven. "I've got to get ready for work." She picked up her cup of tea. "Will you be home this afternoon? The florist and the caterers are coming at five."

Gere was staring into his tea. "I'll be here. Are you going wear that black dress again?"

She stopped in the doorway. "No, I've got a new one for the occasion."

"Not red lace, I hope."

"Of course not." She tried to give him one of those impish smiles Risë did so well. "It's navy lace."

She was right about not having any trouble getting a date. Three men were lined up ready to ask her out when she arrived at the office. One of them was a partner, albeit a junior one. Reed Thomason was a legal wizard, brilliant and cruel in the courtroom. He was Gere's age but his antithesis in appearance and manner: black hair, steel blue eyes, tall and muscular, sartorially smooth, and with a personality as crisp as the pleat in his trousers. Every female in the Financial District had erotic dreams about him. He'd never have any interest in a girl barely out of school, barely more than a clerk, a girl who dressed modestly, a girl who rode the bus, a girl who kept her nose in her own business, whose blue eyes never held any invitation.

Of course, the fact that she had been seen going to break bread with Gere Mackie put her in an entirely new light.

When he caught her in the coffee room, backing her against a wall with his smooth, courtroom style, she had second thoughts about inviting him, but she wanted someone who would impress Risë and Stephen and, perhaps more importantly, Gere.

"Well, Miss Kraft, I think it's about time we got better acquainted," he said in a tone of contemptible familiarity.

"Really?" She stirred her tea, not looking up. "How very flattering."

He ignored the sarcasm, and took a step nearer, stopping just short of invading her personal space. "Oh, that's hardly fair. You're always hiding away in your cubicle, I've never really had a chance to get to know you. Suppose we went out to dinner tonight; I could make it up to you." He warmed up to the idea without waiting for her response. "I know this great little restaurant up the coast-"

"You know," Amanda gave him an ingenuous smile that would someday serve her well in the courtroom, "I'm going to a party tonight at Gere Macke's house. You could come along."

"Gere Mackie?" Reed said the name as if he might have heard it somewhere, sometime but wasn't quite sure. "Oh, right, the reporter."

Amanda saw through the act, but didn't let on. "Yes, he's my…step-brother. We're having a party for our sister. She just got married." She eased away from his proximity and dropped her teabag into the bin. "It's at seven o'clock. I can give you the address, if you're interested," she added casually.

"That sounds like fun," he said, the same way he might find a root canal amusing. "Is it formal?"

"Business formal." Actually, if she knew Gere, he'd be in cargo jeans and a pullover. Risë would come in wearing something new and lavish and then be disappointed because Gere didn't dress up. Stephen would be feeling uncomfortable and overdressed in his rented dinner jacket and complain to Risë about it every time there was a lull in conversation. Oh, yes, it was going to be a fun evening.

"Does that go for women, too?" He touched her shoulder, and she knew he was testing the weight of her grey wool suit. It must have passed the test. "I thought I'd bring flowers. And maybe we could go on somewhere from there."

I don't think so, Amanda thought, but she smiled again. "Navy blue." She could see by the reaction in his eyes that he was envisioning her in a corporate three piece suit. *Boy, was he going to be surprised.*

Gere called after lunch to assure her he was feeling better. His voice still sounded raspy and raw, but his speech was animated, as if he was looking forward to the party. "Did you get a date?"

"Oh, yes." Amanda decided to be cool about it. "One of the partners. Did you?"

"Marita Vele." He matched her tone. "Do you remember her? She's in the ballet company."

Amanda did remember her. She was small, thin, with volumes of black hair and brown eyes that overwhelmed her little oval face. Amanda had only met her a couple of times, but she had the feeling that the heavy, indefinable accent was manufactured. She was disappointed. Reed wasn't going to impress Gere if Gere never saw him through all that hair and accent. "Well, that will be nice. Risë liked her, didn't she?"

Gere laughed. "You must have her confused with someone else. I don't think Risë ever met Marita. Anyway, she's been on tour and she just got back into town. It will be nice to see her again. She'll be her around six thirty to give us a hand with the last minute details." He paused to cough. "Don't pay any attention to that," he warned. "So, when will you be home?"

"Oh, the usual time." Amanda wanted to be as excited as Gere seemed to be, but the closer she got to the party, the more she dreaded it. It was going to be a watershed of some sort, she just knew it. She was having a flash of Risë's insight. Something was going to happen that would change everything. Gere was going to fall in love with Marita. Reed was going to do something to make himself irresistible to her. Gere and Risë would have a fight that would cause them never to speak to one another again. She and Gere would have a fight. Or, worst of all, they would just realize that once Risë was completely out of their lives, they had no life together. She dreaded the evening ahead.

Reed's flowers got there before she did. They were baby white roses, and more suited to a prom than a wedding reception – unless she was the bride. As she entered the apartment, she found Gere frowning at a box in his hand. "Flowers?" he said.

Amanda pretended to be pleased even though she was cringing inwardly. "Oh, how thoughtful." She read the card and cringed outwardly. He was already making assumptions. "Well, that's the way Reed is."

"Reed?" Gere followed her down the hall, nearly cannoning into her when she stopped to watch the caterers setting up. "What kind of name is Reed?"

Amanda shrugged. "The same kind as Gere, I suppose."

Gere drew himself up indignantly. "Gere is French. It's a derivative of guerre, which means war. My father wanted a warrior."

"No, *my* father did. I happen to know you were named in honor of my father. And they both got a warrior," she soothed, patting him on the shoulder. "When Reed gets here you can ask him what his name means."

"Oh, I know what it means," he answered, irritably. "It means redheaded."

Amanda laughed. "That certainly is not Reed Thomason, unless his barber is keeping secrets for him – his hair is so black it's nearly blue. And how would you know, anyway?"

Gere followed her to her bedroom door. "I studied names in college."

"Why on earth would you do that?"

He shrugged. "I needed an easy elective in language. Do you know what Risë means?"

Amanda started unbuttoning her jacket, shaking her head as she did so.

"Laughter. That was for your mother. And doesn't it suit Risë?" He was scowling at her.

At least he's not talking about her in the past tense. Amanda stepped out of her grey suede pumps. "It suits Risë," she conceded, reaching for the shoebox in her closet, "but I can't imagine it being a tribute to *my* mother. She wasn't exactly a comedienne."

"Oh, that's because you didn't know her before your dad came back from El Salvadore," Gere explained quickly. "It definitely suited her then."

"I've heard other people say that. I'm sorry I never saw that side of her," Amanda answered, wistfully. "I wish I knew why she changed."

"Your father changed in El Salvadore. I think I understand, now. You see things in war..." He jerked himself away from the subject. "Your mother was a good, kind, generous woman, Amanda. Just like you. She would be so proud of you." His voice grew crisp. "I think the naming of children is important. It has a lot of bearing on their futures. Do you know what Amanda means?"

She shook her head again.

He backed away from the door." It means worthy of love."

Chapter 8

As promised, Marita came at six. She wore a black Lycra dress with a ballerina neckline, long narrow sleeves, tight bodice, and clinging skirt. She wore no jewelry or make up. She looked like a ballerina – she looked as if she intended that no one mistake her for anything but a ballerina. She floated through the door without knocking, filled with a confidence born of familiarity; as if she knew every corner of the place, and asserted her dominion over it.

Amanda couldn't recall a time when Marita might have been there without herself or Risë there to be hostess, but Marita certainly came in with an air that suggested she was quite comfortable in the role. Coming into the foyer, and shedding her wrap, she hovered, wraith-like, as she took in Amanda's efforts at decoration and food, and was making mental changes to each detail. "Gere?" she called huskily.

Amanda, putting the final touches on flowers in the living room, turned and said, "He's changing." One glance at Marita in her simple elegance and Amanda felt overdone, overdressed, even in her bathrobe. She nodded toward the kitchen, filled with the sounds of the catering staff preparing to set up a buffet. "They'll get you a drink."

"No, thank you." Marita floated (later Amanda would try to call if she ever saw Marita's feet touch the floor) to Gere's door, tapped lightly, and went in.

Open mouthed, Amanda stared, waiting for Marita to emerge, red faced, dismissed from Gere's chambers. She did not appear. Finally, Amanda went down the hall to her own room, to dress.

Amanda had correctly predicted that Gere would not make any special effort with his appearance. He was in varying shades of grey but no variation of comfort: baggy slacks, a collarless pullover with a white tee barely visible beneath. His dark blond hair had been trimmed and slicked back from his face.

When Amanda finished dressing and came out to check on the buffet, Gere was lounging on the sofa, a glass of wine in hand, watching the light fade on the street below, Marita coiled up on the floor at his feet.

He turned as she entered, watching her move around the table, double checking placement of dishes. "Nice dress," he called.

Marita turned, looked at her and turned away, uninterested.

Amanda fingered the navy lace. The dress had long sleeves, a Victorian collar, a long handkerchief hem. She liked it. She thought it emphasized the best features of her figure, her long legs, narrow waist and straight shoulders. "Thanks." She flicked a glance at Marita, curled on the floor, her dainty (invisible) feet tucked under her. She oozed confidence and grace.

"Where are your flowers?" he drawled, handing the glass to Marita and standing.

"In the kitchen." Amanda rearranged the napkins – pale pink with silver bells – keeping the table between them. It was childish, it was gauche, it showed a lack of confidence and grace, but she couldn't stop shaking when Gere got near her, and for some reason, he seemed determined to be near her. "I'll let Reed put them on when he gets here." She backed up a step or two and found her breath again. "It's the correct thing to do."

"And Amanda always does the correct thing." Gere followed her around the table, idly touching the small glass bells filled with chocolates meant to serve as gifts for the guests. "Are you all right? Your hands are shaking." He caught one before she could retreat any further.

"I'm fine," she insisted, trying to ease her hand from his.

He released her. "You can't stand to have me touch you," he hissed.

Amanda shot an anxious glance toward the kitchen. "You're imagining things."

"Am I?"

"Yes," she laughed weakly. "Now go back to your guest. That's also the correct thing to do." She could feel Marita's interest rising.

"In a minute." Gere's was voice was rising, too. "Why can't you stand still when I come near you?"

"Well, for Heaven's sake, why are you so determined to come near me?" Amanda blurted. Over Gere's shoulder, she could see Marita stand and float toward them. "Gere, please, let's not have an argument now. People are coming."

"Let them come. I want this resolved, here and now." He pointed to the floor between them. "You're not going to forgive me, are you? Not now, Marita," he snapped as the ballerina put a hand on his shoulder.

"But, *mijito*, you should not let your sister upset you before a party," she purred with her invented accent. "It is bad for the digestion." She pointed a pencil thin finger at Amanda. "And you are a bad sister to start a fight now."

"She's not-" Gere stopped himself, pulling free of Marita's touch, grabbed Amanda's hands and propelled her back into the hall to her bedroom, forcing her to sit at the edge of her bed. Shutting the door behind him, he put his weight against it, folded his arms across his chest and met her astonished eyes. "Well? Do you want to tell me about it?"

Amanda tried to smile, saw it wouldn't work and sighed. "There's nothing to tell. Honestly, Gere, there's nothing. I admit I'm a little nervous right now but that's normal."

"Normal? How is it normal? Do you mean the party tonight? Having Marita here? How is it normal?"

"Well, yes, the party tonight. And…and I'm dating someone new and…" she sighed. "And everything's new. Everything's changing. I'm feeling a little off balance."

"Everything's changing," Gere repeated glumly, "and I changed it. You're never going to feel safe or comfortable with me again."

"Oh, good grief, Gere," she protested. "You didn't beat me up, or – or rape me-"

Gere shuddered. "Don't even suggest such a thing. If you had seen what I have seen…" He closed his eyes as if to shut out images burned on his memory. "No, never mind, I don't even want you to know about those things."

"Gere," Amanda said gently, "we're not that sheltered. We read, we watch the news. We know what's happening there."

He reached for her but pulled back. "I don't know. With Risë eloping and you and I estranged like this, I feel like I've lost a huge part of myself."

Amanda laughed, grimly. "We've got our roles reversed, Gere. I'm the one who should be frightened by the change in you - you're supposed to be brushing it aside, saying it's no big thing."

Gere's eyes darkened in pain. "Do you see frightening changes in me?" he asked quietly.

Amanda put her hands up to stop him. "You've been through something terrible, more terrible than I'll ever understand. It's natural that it would affect you."

"You *do* think I've changed."

She sighed helplessly. "Of course, but that doesn't mean-"

"I've had…maybe five significant relationships in fifteen years," he told her, as if that should count for something.

She gaped. "What does that have to do with-"

"Everything." He raised his voice. "Everything. I don't get close to people. I don't invest in relationships…not even for sex."

She put her hands to her ears. "I shouldn't be hearing this."

He crossed the room and pulled her hands down. "I want you to hear this. Even in college I didn't have one night stands. It was so…empty."

"What about that Presidential aide?" Amanda asked with narrowed eyes.

"Presidential..." Gere blushed. "I was joking, Amanda. It's too dangerous to fall into bed with strangers."

"Well, what about Marita?"

"Oh, Marita." Gere rolled his eyes. "I don't even know why I invited her. She's so…do you know she just waltzed into my bedroom this evening, unannounced and uninvited?"

Amanda stood. "Gere, you don't have to justify your love life to me. It's none of my business. None of it." She made herself pat his shoulder. "Go ahead and enjoy Marita's company. It won't upset me or make me jealous. Now, let's go. We're going to have company any moment." The strange turn in the conversation bewildered her, and was possibly more frightening than his behavior the night before.

Gere moved away from the door, reluctantly. "I just want you to understand that no one else would notice changes in me, Amanda. And if what I see as a little jumpiness scares you this much, then maybe there's something I don't see. And if you can't stand to be alone in a room with me, maybe I should leave. This is your home."

Home. Why did such a simple word incite such melancholy in her? Because, for the first time in thirteen years, she felt as if she didn't have a home. Amanda willed herself not to tear up and she smiled and said, "Of course, Gere."

Gere's face was a mask of pure disbelief, and he might have expressed it, but the doorbell rang. He stepped forward and let her open the door.

Marita had opened the door by the time they came down the hall and was greeting Risë and Stephen as if welcoming strangers into her home. Seeing Amanda, Risë bounded past her and grabbed her by the shoulders, swinging her around. "I am so happy," she whispered. "He is so wonderful."

Stephen ambled in behind his bride. To his credit, he didn't give Marita a second glance, but his smile was smug when he greeted Amanda, a little tilt to his head saying 'You see what you could have had?'

Amanda accepted his embrace with gritted teeth.

Behind them, Gere came into the dining room. "Risë," he said warmly, holding his arms out for a hug.

Risë turned to him and her smile faded. She looked ashamed, alarmed, unsure. "Gere."

Gere looked as if he couldn't have been more hurt if Amanda and Risë had spent the day shooting him with his father's high powered hunting rifles. It took him a moment to pull himself together and then he made his smile bright. "So? How's married life?"

"Fine," Risë said, carefully.

"Great," Stephen added with more enthusiasm. "You should try it, old man."

Risë and Amanda looked at one another and then at Gere, waiting for some telltale response like a blush, a stammer, a confession. He merely smiled politely, and said, "Oh, I plan to someday."

Marita floated into the dining room, waving Gere's glass of wine. "Hello, hello. Happy wedding!"

"Thank you." Risë smiled, bewildered. When Marita opened the door, her demeanor had been cool and haughty, and now she seemed to be pouring on charm. Risë looked at Amanda with raised brows, seeking identification.

Amanda nodded to let her know that she would tell all later. She was more interested in watching Stephen to see if he would ogle her now that he was seeing her in better light, but apparently the light only shone on Risë. He just patted Risë's shoulder and repeated, "Thanks."

They were saved from the awkwardness of the moment by the doorbell. Mutual friends of Gere, Risë and Amanda arrived, bearing silver wrapped gifts and felicitations. The party was officially begun.

With Risë as one of the guests of honor, it fell to Amanda to be hostess, which left her imagination free to wander. It seemed to wander as far as the conversation in her bedroom and no farther. Why had he felt he needed to tell her about his romantic and sexual relationships? Had he somehow sensed that latent longing in her and was trying to tell her he wasn't interested? Was it really just to show that only she knew him well enough to know something was wrong? Or was it just one more strange and out of character action he had taken recently?

Reed arrived late. Amanda had forgotten about him. The group of two dozen guests had spit pretty much along gender lines, with the women in the living room relating wedding stories, and the men clustered around the buffet in the dining room. Marita was the only dissenter, clinging to Gere's arm with determination.

Reed's arrival drew attention, primarily from the women, as he breezed in, looking over Amanda's head in search of celebrity. He wasn't disappointed. There were several faces from the television screen. Only after he spotted Gere pouring wine for a buddy from the network did he deign to acknowledge Amanda's presence. He kissed the air somewhere near her cheek and said, "Nice dress." He then gave her a more critical look. "Where are the flowers?"

"Oh!" Amanda put a hand to her cheek, embarrassed. "They're in the kitchen. I was waiting for you. This way." She led the way through the dining room. "We can do introductions in a minute," she promised.

Amanda wasn't sure but she felt that he was taking an extraordinarily long time pinning the corsage in place. She felt silly even wearing flowers, after all, she wasn't the bride. But, Reed seemed determined that she observe the old fashioned custom, so she stood still and let him fuss with the pin.

During the process, Gere wandered into the kitchen with a handful of empty bottles, his fake smile still in place. "So, AJ, are you going to introduce us?"

Reed jerked around eagerly at the sound of that famous voice, jabbing the pin into Amanda's flesh. "Gere Mackie, I'd know you anywhere." He held out a hand. "Let me just say what a pleasure it is to meet you."

Gere never bothered to make eye contact. "Nice to meet you, too." He released his hand and came toward Amanda, who was trying, discreetly to remove the pin and put the flowers on without drawing blood. "I hope you're not a surgeon," he chuckled, taking the corsage and slipping the pin into place smoothly and easily. "Are you okay, honey?"

Amanda nodded. "Gere, this is Reed Thomason. He's with the firm where I work."

"Bond, Walker & Phills" Reed supplied proudly.

"Yes," Gere said, dryly, "I know where Amanda works. You'd better come along, AJ, Risë's eager to get into the loot everyone brought. Oh, you, too…er…Thomason."

Reed looked slightly aghast. "Amanda," he whispered. "Should I have brought a gift?"

"Oh, no." Amanda was wondering, once again, why she had invited this self important mannequin to the party, but as she had she forced herself to be polite. "Would you like a glass of wine?"

"I would." Reed suddenly turned solicitous and it wasn't hard to guess why. He had seen that Gere valued his 'step-sister'. "Could I get you a glass, too?"

Risë and Stephen had very generous friends. Every time wrapping paper tore it was followed by Risë's genuine squeal of delight. Everyone looked happy and well fed. The party could be called a success, except for the longing and hurt that passed between Risë and Gere every time they looked at one another. Every time Amanda saw one looking at the other, her heart broke a little.

Risë had confided that she and Stephen were leaving for London on Sunday morning, and Amanda couldn't bear for Risë and Gere to part on such distant and disturbing terms. As people began to gather their coats and begin the goodbyes and well wishes, Amanda pulled Risë aside. "I won't see you for such a long time. Come back tomorrow and we'll have brunch, just the four of us and say goodbye properly, without a lot of outsiders."

Risë shot a glance toward Gere, who was trying to accept the congratulations of a colleague, his plastic smile still plastered in place. "I don't know, Amanda. I don't think Gere's forgiven me for the way all this happened."

"Of course he has. You're his sister. He loves you. He only wants your happiness. Come back tomorrow and assure him that you'll be happy."

"I told him I was happy," Risë argued, still watching her brother, her eyes filled with sorrow. "I told him on the phone last week. I told him when we came to get the rest of my things. I told him tonight. He just doesn't want to believe me."

"He will," Amanda promised. "He just needs to get used to the idea. Give him time," she urged, squeezing Risë's hand. "He'll be happy for you. He will. It's just hard for him to realize that his little sister is all grown up and doesn't need him to protect her anymore." She gave Risë a watery smile. "He's been through so much, Risë, you've must have noticed that he's not quite himself right now. I think everything bothers him a little more than normal."

Risë nodded, slowly. "I thought it was my imagination," she whispered. "It's as if there's something simmering inside him, and it might boil over any minute. Are you all right here with him?"

Amanda wondered, briefly, if she was. It hadn't occurred to her, even after the events of the night before, that she might be in danger, but now even Risë seemed concerned..."Oh, I'm fine. He just needs our patience and understanding." She squeezed Risë's hand once more. "Please say you'll come tomorrow. Don't let it end like this."

Risë hugged her. "I won't. Thank you, Amanda. I probably never told you this and I should have said it a hundred times. You're the best sister a girl ever had."

"Oh, Risë," Amanda sighed, her voice full of tears. "I'm going to miss you so much. Please be happy."

"Come on, now, let me get in on all the hugging," Stephen insisted.

As Amanda backed away and said a stiff and formal goodbye to Stephen, Gere was suddenly at her side, his hand on her shoulder. Stephen looked at him, amused. "Calm down, old man," he advised with that irritating grin, "I'm not going to steal her off, too. And you needn't worry about your baby sister. Amanda's made it clear as rain water what will happen if I make Risë unhappy." He bent over Amanda's extended hand a pressed a kiss to it.

Gere's eyes were frowning, even as he emulated Stephen's grin. "Actually, I'm not a bit afraid of you doing anything to disturb me. Amanda's too clever be taken in by your act, as I'm sure you've already discovered." He paused, significantly. "And Risë's quite capable of making your life miserable if you cross her, so I'd never need to lift a finger in that direction. Actually, I just needed Amanda's attention because I need to ask her something, so," he took the hand that Stephen continued to hold, "if you'll excuse us." He pulled Amanda away and down the hall.

Amanda didn't know whether to be amused that he was trying to protect her from Stephen's dubious charm or be concerned because he had something dire to announce. Bewildered, she looked at him as he backed her against her bedroom door. "Gere, what is it?"

"I just wanted to tell you that I'm taking Marita back to her hotel. I…" he hesitated, uncomfortable, "may not be back tonight."

Amanda nearly laughed at his expression. The only thing that kept the laughter contained was a peculiar pain that caused her heart to swell. Why should it disturb her that Gere wanted to spend the night with that dark wraith? "Well, Gere, I did tell you to enjoy her. Wait. If you want to stay here, I can-"

"No, that's all right." Gere threw a glance down the hall where Reed stood, near the door, with yet another drink in hand, watching them. "I'll see you in the morning."

"What time will you be back? Risë and Stephen are coming for brunch." She lowered her eyes, embarrassed. "I just thought you'd like to say goodbye to her in a less public way."

"You're very sweet." Gere placed a light kiss on her brow and backed away from her. "Goodnight."

Amanda followed him a moment later, wondering if this new, unexplained sadness was apparent in her expression. Gere was tenderly laying a slinky ruanna over Marita's narrow shoulders, as she smiled up at him, possessively. That smile hurt more than anything else she had endured in the last few weeks.

Chapter 9

As Marita and Gere left the apartment, Amanda turned to Reed, expectantly. The only sounds in the apartment were the clatter of dishes as the caterers finished clearing up, and the deep, friendly boom of the fog horn. She looked toward the door, and back at Reed again. Why was he just standing there, sipping from his glass? Why wasn't he collecting his coat, thanking her for the invitation and saying goodnight?

He smiled at her. "This is a nice place you have here."

"It's not mine," Amanda countered.

He wasn't listening. "Good neighborhood, great view, very homey." He sipped. "Although, I always figured him for something flashier: high rise, high tech, luxury bachelor pad. This is more of a family home."

"It is their family home." Amanda rubbed her lace covered arms, in agitation. "Well, it was-"

"Ah, that explains it." He wandered into the living room, pausing before a wall of photographs. It was an impressive montage. Gere had arranged it himself. There were pictures of Gere and Risë with their parents.

There were some of Risë and Amanda as they grew up. There were many of Gere on assignment in some exotic place. Soon a picture taken in a chapel in Reno would be given a place of honor, although, at the moment it was wrapped in tissue paper and lying on Amanda's bed. "Your step-sister is cute, too. That's some stiff she married, though."

Amanda shrugged. She had to agree with his assessment, but to admit that to anyone, even Reed, would be traitorous to Risë.

"I get the feeling this was not a marriage sanctioned by big brother." Reed glanced over his shoulder. "Am I right?"

"Gere and Stephen have known each other for years. They're like brothers," Amanda lied.

"If he wasn't before, he is now. So," he put the glass down, "shall I see you home?"

Amanda panicked. She didn't want Reed to know where she lived. She had a feeling it could pose problems in the future. "No, thanks. It's not necessary. I have to stay until the caterers are through cleaning up."

"Okay." He hitched his slacks and sat. "I can wait."

Amanda sent a worried glance toward the dining room, wishing the catering team wasn't half so efficient. "It could take a while."

"That's okay," he said, easily. "No work tomorrow." He patted the sofa beside him. "Sit down. Relax. You've been on edge all night. It's time you got to have a little fun."

Amanda circled the room and paused before the big recliner in the far corner. It was old and incongruous with the rest of the furnishings, but it had belonged to Risë and Geer's father and now it was Gere's chair. By unspoken agreement, Risë and Amanda avoided contact with it, as if it were a sacred shrine. But, it was also the chair farthest from Reed. She sat down.

Reed frowned. "You know, for a while, there, I thought you liked me."

Amanda laughed nervously. "Of course I do. That is, I suppose I do. I don't know you very well."

Reed's smile was almost serpentine. "Wouldn't you like to get better acquainted?"

She nodded, enthusiastically. "Absolutely. Tell me about yourself." This was something Risë had taught her: All men loved to talk about themselves.

Reed opened his mouth as if to embark on a great oratory, paused and frowned again. "That's not what I meant," he chided.

Amanda smiled demurely. "It's what *I* meant."

"Oh, I get it." Reed nodded to himself and began to rise.

Amanda's hopes began to rise at the same time. He was leaving at last.

But he came to the chair, took her hands and pulled her to her feet, sliding his hands up her arms, and around her body to hold her close. "The only thing you need to know about me is that I am very attracted to you." He kissed her.

Amanda tried to respond. She almost wanted to be aroused by his touch, but her mind kept comparing his kiss and caress to what Gere's might be. Shocked by such thoughts, she struggled, more against herself than his embrace.

Reed broke contract and backed away, scowling. "What's the matter with you? Why did you invite me to this party if you didn't want to have anything to do with me?"

"*I* invite...it was *your* idea!" Amanda protested. "You asked me out." She felt those tears threaten again. "Besides, I know the only reason you suddenly wanted to 'get to know me better' was because you found out I knew Gere Mackie."

"That's true." Reed didn't even try to act affronted. "But, whatever the reason, I did want to go out with you, so," he shrugged, "what's the big problem? I'm here now, aren't I?"

"And that means I'm supposed to be grateful?" Amanda said coolly. "Because I didn't get that memo. Sorry to disappoint you, Mr. Thomason, but I have standards."

Reed's face darkened with anger, and for a moment Amanda expected him to whirl around and exit like an enraged diva, furiously vowing to make her life at Bond, Walker & Phills a living hell. But his expression softened. He gave her his soothing-the-jury smile. "Oh, dear, Amanda, we really got off on the wrong foot. Come on, let's start over." He indicated the sofa, suggesting they sit together, but Amanda remained standing. "The truth is I noticed you a long time ago; finding out you were related to Gere Mackie just gave me an excuse to approach you. Let's face it, Amanda, you do tend to keep yourself removed from everyone socially." He touched her shoulder and gave her a coaxing smile. "So, let's get to know one another. I think you'll like me if you get to know me."

I couldn't possibly like you as much as you like yourself, Amanda thought. Reed, she realized, was a paper doll. Good looking, but two dimensional. She wanted a man with depth, with substance. Even Stephen O'Hara, with his greedy, womanizing manners, had substance, albeit sticky and somewhat unpleasant. Gere was a man with depth. *Why am I suddenly comparing Reed to Gere? Why would I compare anyone I dated to Gere? When did I start thinking of Gere as more than a big brother? When did I start thinking of Gere as a man?*

"Amanda?" Reed touched her shoulder again. "Is something wrong?"

"Hmm?" She focused on him. "It's nothing."

Reed tried to pull her close. "Then why don't we start getting to know one another?"

She twisted free, exasperated. "Reed, your idea of getting to know someone is more...Biblical than mine."

Reed shook his head with a rueful smile. "I would never have taken you for a prude."

"I'm not a prude!" she said hotly. "I just don't believe in rushing into relationships."

"All right, all right." Reed's voice was tolerant and patronizing. "You don't want to be known as a pushover. Don't worry, I'll still respect you."

"Oh!" Amanda backed up but she had nowhere to go. This man was worse than Stephen. He was slime in a three hundred dollar suit.

"Amanda, relax." Reed was laughing as he caught her shoulders before she stumbled over the recliner. "It's not that big a deal."

Before she could assure him that he was the one making it a big deal, a girl in a black and white uniform appeared at the dining room door. "Excuse me, Miss, we're ready to go."

Amanda broke free and hurried to get her check book from her bag. She wrote the check slowly, chatting with the girl, not wanting the young woman and her two assistants to depart and leave her alone with Reed. But it was past midnight and the caterers were eager to be gone. As the door shut on caterers and their equipment, Amanda stood in the hallway, trying not to be wring her hands in anxiety.

Reed watched the door close and he smiled triumphantly. "Well, I see you home, now."

Amanda shook her head. "That's not necessary, Reed. I'll wait for Gere-"

"It's going to be a long wait." Reed was strolling toward her, slowly, but with purpose. "I heard that ballerina invite him back to her hotel room and he agreed."

"How did you know that she was a ballerina?" Amanda demanded, hoping to sidetrack him.

"I heard her tell just about everyone here," he said, sarcastically.

"Oh, the way you make sure everyone knows you're a partner," Amanda countered.

"You know, Amanda, I'm really starting to think you don't like me," Reed said with mock sadness. "And that's too bad because it would make working together so unpleasant."

"That sounded like a threat," Amanda said, eyes narrowing.

"Me threaten you?" Reed feigned innocence. "I'm a lawyer, baby. I know better than to leave myself open to a threat of sexual harassment." The innocence turned evil in a blink.

The message was clear: cooperate or he would find some way to get her discharged that would leave no room for legal retribution. It would have given Amanda a great deal of pleasure to quit right there, but then what would she do? There would be no way to get decent references out of Bond, Walker & Phills. And she needed a job, especially since she was on the verge of ending her relationship with Gere and the home he provided. She tried to smile, even though her lips were numb. "I think you're deliberately trying to mis-understand me, Reed. It's not a matter of liking or disliking you. It's just a matter of timing."

"Fine. Let's go back to your place and discuss it." He had her backed against the hall closet door the same way Gere had trapped her against her bedroom door, earlier. "What do you say, Amanda?"

"Did you hear that creaking sound?" Amanda pushed against him. "The caterers must have left the back door open or something. I'd better go and check."

Reed's grip on her shoulders tightened enough to make her squeal. "Stop fooling around, Amanda."

"Reed, I'd advise you to get your hands off me," Amanda told him in as level and non-threatening voice she could manage. "You're leaving bruises that would be very difficult to explain away."

"You bitch," he hissed.

"No, just someone capable of saying no and meaning it." She gave him a little push, but he didn't move. "And I mean it."

"You won't get away with it."

"I'm not trying to get away with anything. I just don't want you getting away with anything, either. Now, let me go."

It was his turn, once again, to change directions. "Whoa, now, we're getting way off track here. All I wanted to do was take you home."

"There's no reason to take her home."

Amanda looked over Reed's shoulder. "G-Gere, what are you doing here?"

Reed froze, and then backed away from Amanda, hands shoved in pockets, trying to put a welcoming smile on his face before he turned around.

Gere was smiling but his eyes were absolutely blazing. "You want to tell me what's going on here, fella?"

"Gere, it's just a-"

Gere put a hand up. "Wasn't talking to you, AJ. I asked the lawyer. Why did you have her backed up against a wall, with a grip that made her cry out? Why were you using that tone of voice and those words on a nice young lady? Why were you trying to take her someplace she obviously didn't want to go? That's not very nice."

"Look, Gere," Reed began, trying to smooth his shaky voice with oil.

"Call me Mr. Mackie," Gere interjected.

That disconcerted him. "Mr. M-Mackie, it's not a big deal. I just wanted to see my date home, that's all." Reed tried smiling, and it was pathetic. He wanted desperately to remain in the good graces of a man whose step-sister he had been caught manhandling. There just wasn't a legal precedent for that.

"There's no need to take her anywhere. She lives here." Gere looked Amanda as if to ask why she didn't tell him that.

"Here?" Reed turned around to ask her the same question with a very different look.

"I think it's time we all said goodnight." Gere's voice, the same one he used with related facts while bullets flew around him and bombs burst over his head, was calm and unflappable, but determined. "Oh, and by the way, Mr. Thomason," Gere put a hand on Reed's arm and apparently exerted a little pressure, "Amanda likes her job. She expects to go far with Bond, Walker & Phills so she'd better work there a long, long time. Because if she doesn't," he stepped forward and dropped his voice to a friendly whisper, "she's going to sue you for harassment, and I'd give excellent testimony, since I heard everything you said to her."

Reed spluttered and lost what little control he had. "And you think your word would be enough to-"

"Oh, it wouldn't be just my word" Gere interrupted. "There would be the word of the caterer who met me outside as I was pulling up and told me that you appeared to be bothering Amanda and she appeared to be concerned about being alone with you. There would be an entire room full of press who would testify that you drank heavily through the evening and stared at Amanda inappropriately all night. Then there's the matter of the bruises she's going to have – a few photographs and a doctor's report would be very compelling evidence, don't you think?"

Gere dropped his arm around Reed's shoulders and gave him a fraternal squeeze. "Let me paint you a picture. Suppose you drum up cause to discharge her or harass her until she leaves and she sues you. Your firm can only handle it one of two ways; you fall on your sword and settle out of court, thereby forever tainting you and your firm, or you take her to court and try to bull your way through it. If her case went in front of a jury – and I'll make certain that it did – who do you think the jury's going to listen to? The oily shyster with his fabricated smile and expensive suits or the honest, humble, hardworking reporter they've listened to for ten years?"

He slapped Reed on the back. "I have a high level of credibility right now because I got kidnapped in a war zone and managed to escape. If I got on the stand and told them you flew to Mars and back, it would be the same as if it led the six o'clock news. So, don't try anything stupid, okay?" He pulled the door open for the floundering attorney. "Goodnight."

Amanda was still standing with her back against the closet door, her mouth open. She'd never seen Gere so cocky, or so mean. When

Gere turned around, smiling to himself, she blurted out, "What are you doing here? I thought you were spending the night with Marita?"

He shrugged out of his coat. "I changed my mind. I remembered what I had said to you about one night stands, and that's all this would be." He draped the coat across the back of a chair. "And besides, there was something about the way that guy was watching you all night that made me uncomfortable and I decided to come back and make sure he left like a good little boy."

"He left like a squashed bug on someone's shoe," Amanda observed.

Gere chuckled. "Are you all right?"

"I'm mad as anything but that will pass."

"You should have quit when he first threatened you," Gere said, flipping the lock into place.

"Why should I? I do like my job." Amanda rubbed her shoulder. "And, anyway, whether I like it or not, I need my job."

"You don't need one that bad, honey." He put an arm around her waist. "Do you want to go to the Emergency Room and get those bruises documented?"

"They won't even show for a few hours." She stalled. "Wait, how did you know how hard he was squeezing me? How did you know he threatened me?"

"I heard him. I heard you make a sound of pain."

"How did you get in?"

"I came in the back door. The caterers were just coming down the front steps as I came across the street, and the woman told me he was still here and they were a little worried about the way he was acting. I decided I'd better be discreet in case you two...anyway, I was sneaking in when I heard him threaten you. I got mad. I waited in the dining room a minute to cool off or I would have..." He shook his head. "Why didn't you tell him you lived here?"

"I didn't want him to know where I lived. I thought it might cause trouble in the future, the way he had been acting. If he knew where I slept, he might have spent the entire time to guide me into the bedroom instead of out the front door." She found herself in front of the bathroom door. "Well, thanks for the rescue."

"I didn't rescue you, you were doing fine," Gere countered. "I just showed up to make it clear you had witnesses."

"Thank you for the witness." She flicked on the bathroom light. "Goodnight."

Gere started to say something, but words seemed to fail him. "Goodnight."

Amanda turned on the tap, unzipped and stepped out of her dress, got out her skin care products and began to clean her face.

"Hey, what time are Risë and Stephen coming-" Gere had pushed his way into the bathroom and now stood frozen, looking at Amanda in her navy camisole, tap panties and thigh high stockings. For a moment, he was frozen, unable to speak or retreat, or even move his eyes from her. "I'm sorry," he managed, backing out, awkwardly. "I didn't realize. I'm sorry." He pulled the door shut behind him.

Amanda let her breath out on an unsteady sigh. That had to be the single most horrible moment of her whole horrible day. And the horrible part wasn't that she had been embarrassed that Gere had seen her in her under things. No, the horrible part was that she wanted him to swoop her up, carry her back to his bed and divest her of her under things.

She splashed cool water on her face and pulled her bathrobe down from the hook on the back of the door. When she stepped out into the hall, she could hear Gere in the kitchen, making bottles and glasses clink as he prepared a drink. She shook her head as she went back to her room. He should have stayed with Marita tonight.

Chapter 10

If there had been a film crew in the Mackie kitchen that Saturday morning, they would have believed they were filming a situation comedy. Amanda and Gere were trying to prepare the kind of elegant and festive brunch that Risë loved, working in concert, yet going to extraordinary lengths not to look at each other or come in contact with one another. Their conversations were limited to 'would you fix the...?' and 'please pass the...' In the hour that it took to get everything just right, they had exchanged less than two dozen words.

Amanda wanted to discuss the situation, to talk about what was happening between them, how the dynamic had changed so horribly since Risë's departure, yet she was terrified that Gere would open the subject. After all, how could she explain how her view of him had changed when not filtered through Risë and the family atmosphere that had existed until now? She understood that Gere had drawn a box in the sand, probably desperate to maintain some sense of normalcy in the wake of all he had lost, and now he was stuck. Of course, sooner or later he would step over the line, or allow it to get smudged, and then the situation would resolve itself. Perhaps it was best just to remain silent on the matter and let it fade away.

Of course, in the meantime, she needed to get prepared. She needed to see someone about her much lauded but not so impressive trust fund, she needed to find her own place and she needed to put together enough money to make the move without completely depleting her savings.

"What time will they be here?"

Amanda, standing hands on hips, staring out at the dining room, was roused from her mental wanderings. "Around ten." She actually looked at the dining room table, then. She had used Risë's favorite china and linens, and sent Gere down to the flower vendor on the corner to get her favorite flowers. The effect was very nice, and far more formal than any family gathering they'd ever had.

"It looks beautiful. Risë will be very pleased," Gere promised.

Amanda checked her watch. "I'm going to change."

"Change? What's wrong with what you're wearing?"

They were both wearing similar ensembles – faded, denims, oversized pullovers and running shoes. "It doesn't exactly go with that, does it?" She waved a hand toward her efforts in the dining room. "You're not going to wear that, are you?"

"What's wrong with this?" He tugged at his shirt. "I've dressed this way every Saturday of my adult life. I refuse to put on the dog just because my sister is coming over for breakfast."

"But, you dressed up last night when she came for dinner," Amanda reminded him.

He waved it away. "We were having a party. This is…" he looked at the table. "I don't know what this is."

"Gere," she said softly, feeling her heart break a little more, "this is goodbye for who knows how long. Remember that, won't you?"

Gere frowned, still looking at the table. "What does that mean?"

"It means bend a little." Amanda touched his arm. "Forgive her for abandoning you."

His eyes slid to her fingertips and for a moment, Amanda thought she saw the glistening of tears. "You know, that is exactly how I feel," he confessed in a sad, quiet voice. "I spent so many days and nights thinking about this…" he lifted his eyes to the ceiling, "this place, this life. All I wanted was to get out of there alive and come back here. It was safety, it was a haven, it was normal and comfortable, and, oh, my God, I missed it. Then I came home and everything was undone." He paced a little, putting himself out of her reach, fiddling with forks and spoons. "We had a nice, comfortable life here, the three of us, and she left it with no warning. She destroyed it."

"Destroyed it?" Amanda was started by the anger in those last three words. "That's a little harsh, Gere."

"It is destroyed. It will never be the same." He met her eyes. "You've got it in your head that you're not welcome here anymore. And I'm going out of my way making everyone miserable." He drew a deep breath and shook himself. "All right. I will be warm and kind and supportive when they get here. But, I am not changing."

Amanda relaxed and surrendered the point. "Fair enough. I won't either. Oh, Gere, you've gotten these place settings all out of order." She began rearranging flatware because she didn't know what else to say to him.

Gere watched her, tugging at his lower lip as his eyes followed her around the table. "Amanda, did I ruin things between you and Perry Mason last night?"

Amanda dropped the handful of spoons and forks, staring at him. "No! Whatever would give you an idea like that? There were no 'things' to ruin."

He shrugged. "I've been thinking about it and I guess I might have overreacted. I've been doing that a lot lately. I saw a therapist who said it's common…" he paused to choose his words carefully, "under circumstances like mine." He rubbed his brow. "I saw him backing you against a wall and making threats and I didn't think twice. It's the big brother in me, I suppose."

Big brother. Amanda forced an expression of appreciation. "It's a good thing you didn't take any time thinking it through. I'm not really equipped to deal with these sorts of situations. They don't come up all that often."

"You were doing fine. Risë's the one who always needs rescuing. She gets herself into these situations and then turns into a puddle of panic."

"She didn't get *into* a situation, Gere. She got *into* a marriage."

He ignored her. "You, on the other hand, stand up for yourself. You're the least puddle like woman I've ever seen. You would have put that as-jerk in his place without my help. You just hadn't gotten to it yet."

Amanda smirked. "Regardless of your faith in me, I'm not exactly a *femme fatale*. No one in that office paid much attention to me until word got out that I knew you. I've never really needed to hone my skills."

Gere was making a face. "From what I saw when I got back last night, he didn't seem to be too concerned who you were related to."

Amanda nearly said 'I'm not related to you' but held her tongue. As long as he continued to think of her as one of his girls she would be welcome in his home. Still, if he really did look on her as one of his sisters, then the way he looked at her the night before, when he interrupted her toilette was positively indecent. "All the more reason to thank you for your intervention." She shivered. "It makes me uneasy just thinking about facing him on Monday morning."

"Why should you be uneasy?" Gere demanded. "He's the one who should be ashamed to face you."

"Well, it doesn't work that way," Amanda said, matter of factly. "He'll find a way to spin this, despite your warnings. Judging by his past performances, by Monday noon, word will be all around the office that the great and benevolent Reed Thomason took mousy Amanda Kraft on a pity date, she got over amorous and he had to rebuff her."

"Mousy?" Gere was astonished and indignant. "You're anything by mousy."

Amanda smiled. "Thanks, but that's the big brother in you doing the talking."

Gere cocked his head to one side. "At the risk of upsetting you all over again, that's the man in me talking."

As Amanda struggled with a response the doorbell rang.

Gere gave her an unexpected grin. "Saved by the bell."

"Who could that be?" Amanda followed him into the foyer.

"Risë and Stephen, I assume." He nodded toward the mantel clock. "It's nearly ten o'clock."

"Why would Risë ring the bell?"

Gere reached for the door. "Because she doesn't live here anymore." He put on a ridiculously big grin to pull the door open. "Oh."

Amanda got on tiptoe to look over his shoulder. It was an enormous arrangement of red roses. "Oh."

Gere took the vase and tipped the delivery girl, leaving Amanda to sign for them. "They're for you," he announced carrying them to the living room.

"I didn't think they were for you from Marita." Amanda closed the door. "Not after you dumped her at the hotel last night."

"Marita's the type to expect flowers, not to send them." He plucked the card from its holder and held it out to her.

Amanda scanned the card and looked at the flowers again. "Well, he believes in expensive apologies." She sniffed one deep red bud. "What's the going rate for two dozen long stemmed roses?"

"I have no idea, you mercenary thing." Gere tugged the card from her fingers. "I never have to apologize to women." He read the card. "Do you think I scared him?"

"Maybe." Amanda had never received such an elaborate and elegant arrangement before. She wondered why she wasn't the tiniest bit thrilled.

"Where are you taking them?" Gere asked as she picked up the vase.

"My room. I thought…"

"Oh, leave them out. Give Risë something to wonder about." Gere took the roses from her and put them on the table in the window. "That ought to get her attention. He turned around to find Amada considering them, bemused.

She really thought she ought to be a little bit pleased to get roses.

"You know," Gere said, "anyone can send flowers."

Amanda looked at him, mystified by his remark. "Anyone but you, of course."

"I've sent flowers before," he answered, indignantly. "Just not as an apology."

That was it. There was no thrill in getting a beautiful, expensive bouquet in apology for appalling behavior. It was if he thought he could buy her feelings. She wrinkled her nose at them. The moment Risë and Stephen left, those things were going in the trash.

"There they are," Gere announced. "I recognize Risë's steps on the stairs."

He went to the door again and pulled it open. "Well, hello, strangers," he said brightly.

Risë did not bound through the door with her usual exuberance. She accepted her brother's hug almost indifferently.

Uh oh, Amanda thought, trouble already.

"Amanda." Risë took Amanda's arm and urged her down the hall. "I need to talk to you."

Amanda shot Gere an anxious look as she passed him.

Once inside Risë's former bedroom, looking so empty without the little bits that had defined Risë's personality, Amada looked at her with sisterly sympathy. "What's the matter? What's happened?"

For a moment, Risë only looked at her, her gold eyes large and shiny. "Oh, Amanda," the words rushed out like a bursting dam of emotion. "I'm moving *away*. It all hit me last night when the party was over and I was one of the guests who left. This isn't a game; it's not just a little vacation. I'm moving to a whole new country – to live – to stay!"

Amanda didn't know what to say. The concept of just moving to another apartment was daunting to her. Risë must be terrified. "But, you're not going alone," she said aloud."

Risë looked up. "What?"

Amanda focused on her. "You're not going alone. You have Stephen. He'll be your support and guide."

"Oh, I know." Risë reached automatically for her poodle shaped tissue box, but it was packed in a shipping crate, waiting to go to England. "He's great," she insisted, sniffing. "But, it will be so different. And Stephen's only going to be there at home for a couple of weeks. Then he's going to Moscow on assignment."

"What's so unusual about that?" Amanda asked. "Gere's been on assignments for years."

"I know, but *you* were always here."

Amanda felt an emotional dam of her own about to burst. Everything Risë had ever done to remind her that she did not belong to the family was washed away with that one heartfelt remark. "Oh, Risë," she sighed.

The door pushed open and Gere poked his head in, looking concerned. "What's going on? Should I feed this guy or break his neck?"

"Gere." Risë rushed to him. "Can't Amanda go to England with us? I want Amanda to stay in England with me."

It was a tempting offer: a chance to move before she was asked to leave, a chance to get away from Reed Thomason and the revenge he would eventually wreak on her, and, perhaps most tempting of all, a chance to get away from Gere before she made a very stupid mistake. Before she could put words together, however, Gere surprised them both with a very strident denial. "Don't be ridiculous, Risë. Amanda's not going to give up her life for your comfort. She's got friends and a job and responsibilities here. She can't drop everything to hold your hand through newlywed jitters. Besides, you got your husband. If Amanda leaves, who will I have?" He pushed the door open wide. "Now come out here and eat. Amanda worked very hard to have all your favorites for you." He gave Amanda a furious look as she passed him in the doorway.

❀

The meal started out very stiff and formal, with conversations that were strained and overly polite. But, after Stephen and Gere had liberally availed themselves of the mimosas and then, when the orange juice ran out, plain champagne, both began to loosen up and exchange war stories of their years on assignment.

Risë was uninterested in their tales. She had already heard all of Gere's stories and, as she confided to Amanda, she had her whole life time to hear Stephen's. "Now, tell me the truth," she demanded in an undertone. "How are you? You don't look well. Is everything going okay between you and Gere?"

Amanda shrugged. She hadn't expected Risë to be so perceptive, or even to consider that anything might change in her absence, but this was one thing she couldn't confide in Risë. "Well, he was very upset that you eloped, naturally. It took him a few days to get over that. And he was in Los Angeles for a few days, too."

"So, it's just that I got married? Gere seems so…I don't know…intense. I thought it was about you and that guy you were with – who is a *hunk*, by the way," she added conspiratorially.

"Gere's been a little intense about everything," Amanda said, recalling his words earlier that morning. She debated mentioning his condition, but felt that his sister had a right to know what had been driving his anger – at least in part. "He's seen someone…a therapist. I think it might be something on the lines of Post Traumatic Stress Disorder."

Risë clapped a hand over her mouth.

"He's okay," Amanda said quickly, darting a glance at Gere, who was deep in conversation with Stephen and appeared unaware of them. "He's been through a lot so, really, he's functioning very well."

"Stephen told me some things that Gere didn't tell us," Risë whispered. "That he'd been kept bound and gagged and hooded for several days, and they shot guns around him while he was like that. They stole everything from him, even Grandpa's pocket watch."

Amanda put her hand on Risë's arm. "Don't tell me anymore, please. I can't stand it."

Risë nodded and sat back for a moment. "I noticed the roses. Are they from the hunk?"

Amanda nodded, not yet able to speak past the lump in her throat. How had Gere managed to endure all that?

"My, he has good taste." She twisted around to look at them again. "Maybe Gere was watching you so closely because he's afraid you'll run off with Reed the way I ran off with Stephen." She shook her head, disdainfully. "He really ought to know better. You have more sense than that."

"Implying that you don't?" Amanda protested. "Risë, you've got degrees in sciences I can't even pronounce!"

Risë nodded dismissively. "Yes, yes, I'm smart, but that doesn't mean I have much common sense. Let's be honest, Amanda, when it comes down to what matters, life skills, you got *all* the brains in this family. You'd never run off and marry someone you'd known all of twenty four hours."

"All right, since you brought it up," Amanda leaned toward her again, with voice lowered even more. "Why on earth did you run off with him? I know the version you told everyone last night, but I don't believe in love at first sight, and neither do you. So, let's hear the truth."

Risë met her gaze, unabashed. "I married him because I knew he was determined to take me to bed," she answered frankly. "I gave him my standard rebuttal; I'm saving myself for marriage. And what do you know? He proposed! Look, I know he's nothing but a charmer and a chaser, and he'll probably start running around on me soon enough, but if he does, so what? I'll have fun for a while, maybe get to start a family and…he's very well off, did you know? I'll be settled, at least." When she saw that Amanda was staring at her, dumbfounded by her calculated and callused honesty, she added, "And I couldn't bear the idea of growing into one of those maidenly sisters who lives and dies under brother's care." Risë closed the subject by turning head to tune into the conversation across the table.

"And then, Moscow for who knows how long?" Stephen was toasting Russia with his fifth glass of champagne.

Gere was rocking back on the rear legs of his chair, frowning into his own glass. "What about Risë?"

"She'll be okay," Stephen said, confidently. "She's already told me she plans to spend her first six months in London shopping. And my mum's nearby if she needs anything."

"You'd leave your bride behind in a strange country to go to Moscow on what amounts to your honeymoon?" Gere persisted.

"I wouldn't even think about taking her with me. It's no place for a girl who doesn't consider meat on the table a luxury. What about you?" Stephen reached for the champagne – the second bottle - in the ice bucket. "With all the things happening over there, I'd think you'd be camped right in the middle of Red Square. You're a man who likes to be in the middle of things."

"I don't know." Gere was still frowning into his glass. "I think I've been in the middle of too much lately."

"What's the matter, old man?" Stephen was giggling drunkenly. "Did you lose your nerve with your wallet and watch on this last trip?"

"Maybe." Gere emptied his glass and set it on the table. "Let's see you trade places with me for seven weeks, thinking you were never going to see your loved ones or even daylight again. Let's see how much nerve you come back with."

"I never thought I'd see the day…"

"Maybe I realized I don't have anything to prove anymore and too much to lose."

"Well, I must admit," Stephen paused to pour champagne, "I'd be reluctant to give up a sweet deal like this."

Gere jerked the bottle out of Stephen's hands and pushed the ice bucket out of his reach. "What are you talking about?"

"Well," Stephen's grin was full of innocence and awareness, "this is a nice cozy place for just the two of you." He nodded toward the roses in the bay window. "Romantic view-"

Gere stood, kicking the chair back, taking an offensive stance.

"Stephen!" Risë protested, horrified.

Amanda was too concerned for Risë's feelings to realize that she had been insulted. "Gere, no!" she cried.

Stephen was smiling, woozily, at Gere. "What's this for?"

"I don't like what you're insinuating," Gere said through clenched teeth.

"Why so sore, old man? Am I touching a nerve?" He looked across the table at Risë and Amanda. "Are you trying to tell me that, with little sister carried off to London you haven't fallen into the sweetest deal since we left Kuwait?"

Risë and Amanda exchanged glances. Stephen knew, too!

"Get up," Gere hissed.

"What for? So you can knock me down?" Stephen shook his head. "That drunk I'm not." He shifted his smile to Amanda. "Tell me the truth, Amanda, how many times in the past week has Gere tiptoed down the hall to keep you warm at night?"

Risë put a hand out to Amanda as she started from her chair. "He doesn't mean that."

"That's it." Gere caught Stephen's shirt front and dragged him to his feet. "I don't care if you are my sister's husband. You're a snake and a bastard and you have a filthy mind. I want you out of my house before I tear you limb from limb."

"Gere, please don't do this." Huge tears were rolling down Risë's cheeks.

Amanda slumped into her chair, too miserable to care what Stephen was suggesting. *Poor Risë, how could she have done this to herself? And why did she have to do it to me, too?*

"But first," Gere said, reacting to his sister's tears, "you're going to apologize to Risë for making lewd comments about me and about a woman she regards as a sister. And then I want you to apologize to Amanda for even hinting that she would participate in such an unsavory relationship."

Amanda looked up, stunned. *Unsavory?*

"Unsavory?" Stephen seemed to echo her thoughts. "Look here, old man, what *have* you got going?"

"I'm going to smack you, I swear it." Gere shook him roughly. "Now apologize."

"For what?" Stephen continued to maintain his pose of innocence. "I can't believe that a good looking guy and an attractive girl wouldn't take advantage of a little privacy after all these years. You can't tell me there haven't been sparks before now."

There was no doubt that Gere would have let loose with both fists if the two women hadn't darted around opposite sides of the table and worked their way in between them.

Stephen stumbled back over his chair and ended in a heap on the floor. Gere stood where he was, fists doubled, red faced. "Sparks?" he spat, shoving Risë and Amanda aside to glower threateningly over Stephen's sprawling figure. "She's practically my sister."

Stephen rubbed his temple where he had bumped into something on his way to the ground. "Ah, but she isn't your sister, is she, mate?"

Chapter 11

Amanda shoved the refrigerator door shut, still brushing tears away.

Gere was leaning in the doorway to the dining room, watching her. The slamming front door still echoed around them. "You're really angry, aren't you?"

Amanda tossed a meaningful glare over her shoulder.

"Wait a minute," Gere straightened, looking shocked, "You're angry at me? What did I do?"

"You ruined Risë's last day at home, for a start," Amanda threw the words at him. "You started a fight – an actual, physical fight with her husband."

"I was defending your honor!" he hollered.

"I thought you said I was the one who could handle myself."

"Yes, but-"

"He was drunk. What he was saying didn't mean anything. You certainly have changed, Gere Mackie. Before this, you would have been the first one to use words instead of fists."

He drew back at the suggestion, emotions twitching all over his face before he managed a sullen, "Well, maybe I've learned that sometimes fists get the message across better."

"If that's what you think, you had a poor teacher." Amanda took a tray and inched past him to begin collecting dishes from the table. "I'm really disappointed in you - and embarrassed for you."

"Well," he said huffily, "thanks a lot."

She began stacking dishes carefully. "Even if Stephen had been completely sober, his words shouldn't have upset you so much. You know the truth. I know the truth. That's all that matters." She turned around to look at him. "You hurt your sister very deeply."

"He's the one who hurt her," he argued. "To tell the truth, I'm surprised she left with him."

Amanda's mouth fell open. "For Heaven's sake, Gere, she's married to the man – you know, for better or for worse? It's not the same as a child deciding she doesn't want to play anymore. Risë's not picking up her marbles and coming home." She carried the tray back to the kitchen and began to stack the delicate dishes in the sink full of soapy water. "And I give her full credit for that. It couldn't have been easy for her. Stephen behaved like a boor and you were an ass. She has to be broken hearted."

When she looked over her shoulder, he was still turned toward the dining room. *Why do I bother trying to explain Risë's actions to him?* she wondered. *A man who can walk away from a lover and child might not be able to understand her motivation.* "It's called loyalty, Gere. I admire it."

He turned around. "What's that supposed to mean?"

Amanda shrugged and plunged another glass under the suds.

"Hey." He caught her shoulder and twisted her around. "Are you accusing me of being disloyal?" When Amanda answered with an unblinking stare, he exploded, "I have *never* been disloyal. I've always been there for you and Risë. I've given up a *lot* for you two."

"Oh, no," Amanda jerked free, "don't blame that on us."

"What are you talking about?" He reached for her again, with a not so gentle shake. "Amanda, what is going on?"

As angry as she was, Amanda was still reluctant to fling accusations based on her guilty knowledge. She lowered her eyes and shrugged. "Nothing. I'm sorry, Gere, I'm just upset."

Gere pulled his hands away sharply and tucked them under his arms and paced away from her. "Okay, yeah, I'm getting a little physical. I'm sorry. But, I still don't know what has you so upset." He backed up against the refrigerator, as far from her as he could get and stay in the room. "Look, I'm all the way over here. Now, what is it?"

Amanda opted to lie. "I just wanted Risë's farewell party with us to be perfect."

"Liar." He said it very softly. "You know, Amanda, I think that hurts even more. I don't think you've ever lied to me before."

Amanda resumed her task, blinking away new tears.

"You *are* lying," he repeated, shocked. "Come here." He pulled a chair away from the kitchen table and pointed. "Now."

Amanda had never heard him use that tone of voice before, not even when they were much younger. It scared her that he was even capable such a voice.

Seeing her fear had more impact on him than she expected. The color drained from his face and he settled down in the chair with a thump. "I'm sorry." He covered his face with his hands and sighed heavily. "I don't know what's going on with me." He sat back, his hands dropping to his lap. "Ever since I got back, everything's bubbling up, magnified and out of control. Joy, anger, fear, possessive-ness...it's all out of control."

Amanda came to the table and sat, hesitantly, opposite him. "You should see-"

"-a shrink? I am. I told you I am. The first day I was home...that Saturday before all of this started...part of the debriefing was to be evaluated by someone. I've seen him twice since, and talked to him a couple of times on the phone." He swallowed a couple of times. "This fella says people who've been..."

"Kidnapped?" Amanda supplied. "Taken hostage?"

He answered with a jerk of a nod.

"I understand the effect it had on you, Gere, I really do." Amanda struggled to keep her voice from shaking. "We had a client who...well, he did some pretty bad things and he used his experiences in Iraq as a defense. I did a lot of pre-trial research on it. It's called Post Traumatic Stress Disorder."

Gere smirked grimly. "I've done a little research on it, too. I just never thought it would happen to me."

"Why? Because you're just supposed to report on what's happening? What you see still affects you. Maybe it affects you more because you're expected to be neutral, and you can't take action to change the situation."

"Exactly." He sat back, sighing heavily. "You know, I thought I was tougher than this. I didn't think it would get to me. I've seen some pretty awful things over the years, and I've walked away without looking back, but this…women…kids…" a single tear slipped down his cheek and he sat up sharply and scrubbed at his face. "Anyway, this doctor says there are three ways people who have been kidnapped react once they're released. They can attach themselves to their kidnappers or their kidnapper's cause. Helsinki Syndrome or something like that. Or they become fearful, afraid of everything bad happening, expecting the worst, becoming a victim again when they return to normal life. Or…" he touched his chest, "they become aggressive, angry, pushing back on everything. All emotions are ratcheted up, made larger than the circumstances call for. That's what it feels like, what's happening to me. Anger, happiness, even sexual arous…" his face darkened and he glanced away.

Amanda blushed, too. "What can be done? Did the doctor have any advice?"

"Yes. Therapy. Meds if I want them, which I don't."

"Why not? There's no shame in-"

"Because you can lose your objectivity," he interrupted.

"That's never really been your strong suit," she interjected, wryly.

He shot her a look of frustration. "And you think drugs would help? Anyway, I'm sorry if I frighten you sometimes. I frighten me sometimes." He rapped his knuckles against the table top in agitation. "I don't know if knowing that helps or not."

"Yes. Thank you for telling me. It must have been hard." She started to stand.

His hand whipped forward, grabbing hers. "Wait a minute. I've told you the truth. Now I want the truth. Why are you so angry? You've been angry and upset since before I started exhibiting any after effects. What did I do? What disloyal act do you feel I've committed?"

Amanda sat on the edge of her chair, head bowed, still more tears flowing. "I know about her," she confessed.

"Her?" Gere laughed unexpectedly. "Amanda, you sound like a soap opera. What 'her' are you talking about?"

Amanda had to draw a deep breath to force the confession out. "The girl you left behind in Kuwait – and I know about the baby."

"Baby?" The color was gone again. "How do you know?"

Amanda stared at the brown and yellow tiles of the floor. "Risë found the pictures."

She gestured vaguely in the direction of his bedroom. "She showed them to me the night you...the night everything happened."

Gere sat back in his chair. "And you thought the baby was mine."

Amanda lifted her eyes. "Isn't he?"

"She," he corrected. "Does Risë believe that, too? Oh, obviously, if she showed the pictures to you." He was quiet for a few moments. "Well, I guess that's better than the truth."

"Why? What is the truth?" *And why do I feel so relieved to know that little girl doesn't belong to him?*

Gere rubbed his eyes. "I shouldn't tell you. You and Risë are so close, you're bound to tell-"

Amanda sat up straight with a jerk. "It's Stephen's!"

Gere didn't confirm the fact with so much as a blink, and yet the truth was all over his face. "When we were living Kuwait, Stephen did an interview with a family on how life had changed for them since Desert Storm. People in Kuwait are a little more liberal than other Muslim countries, but there are limits, and Stephen, being Stephen, managed to cross them."

Amanda gasped. "They stone girls for that!"

"They do, but this family didn't. They married her off to someone in Canada right away and put the baby in an orphanage. Kids like that don't stand a very good chance of surviving, much less getting adopted but by this time Stephen had been reassigned. He didn't even know if he had a son or a daughter."

Amanda's heart was breaking. "Where did you get the photos, then?"

"I took them." Gere was obviously struggling with the memories. "I tracked her down and got photos. I thought if Stephen knew about her…" He shook his head. "I tried to figure out a way I could bring her to the States with me. I even tried saying that I was the father, but then they wanted DNA proof and I couldn't come up with it. The best I could do was leave some money for her care at the orphanage. I have no idea if it was actually used for that, but I had no other options and I had to try something.

"Anyway, when I ran into Stephen at the airport in Cypress – I had to sneak out through Greece, it's so chaotic there right now it was easy to get out without my passport and then tell Homeland Security it was stolen in Greece – I told him I had a photograph of Rabi, the girl he'd known in Kuwait. He said he'd come back with me to get it. That surprised me, and suggested that he actually cared for her. Before I could give it to him, however, he'd run off with Risë. After that, I couldn't very well do the big reveal in front of Risë and tell her that she had a five year old step-daughter, could I?"

Amanda brushed tears away with both hands. "You should have beaten him up this morning. I'm sorry I stopped you."

Gere laughed harshly. "No, you were right. Violence wasn't the answer. I just started seeing red when he kept going on and on about what a cozy little life we have here." He looked around the kitchen. "Well, okay, it is a cozy life…it was, at least."

"I know what you mean. It's been a wonderful life." Amanda stood. "Gere, I know that I shouldn't have looked at those pictures, even if Risë did show them to me. I invaded your privacy, and I'm sorry. I'm also sorry that I've been so angry at you all this time for something you didn't do."

Gere gave her a sad half smile. "I suppose it was all right to be angry at me when you thought I had abandoned a child, but I'm surprised you would think I'm capable of that."

Amanda returned to the sink. "Reason would have told me that, if I'd listened. But when we saw that baby's face we just couldn't see any further and reason went out the window." She rinsed a glass. "Risë always intended to ask you, but Stephen distracted her."

"That makes sense, and I really would rather she thought I'd done that instead of the man she married. So, don't feel compelled to set her straight, okay?"

Amanda rinsed the last champagne glass and pulled the plug in the drain. "I wouldn't worry too much about Risë's happiness. You know, I think she went into this marriage with both eyes open."

"What makes you say that?" Gere pulled a cotton dish towel from a drawer and began to dry the glasses while she loaded dishes into the dishwasher.

"She told me today she wasn't in love with him. Her reasons for marrying him were no more starry eyed than his reasons for marrying her. She saw it as a chance to get out and start a life on her own, maybe start a family. She says Stephen's family is well fixed and very happy that he got married."

"Oh, they are," Gere affirmed. "Stephen comes from one of those families that has generations of wealth – like your mother. I was always surprised he worked as hard as he did when he could be living in the lap of high taxed luxury. I guess he's a news junkie to his soul, just like me."

"His similarities to you are very superficial."

He bowed his head. "Thank you."

"Anyway," Amanda began to wipe down countertops, "she figures that if he cheats on her she'll still be ahead in the bargain. She'll have her family and she'll get a pretty good settlement from him if they divorce. This wasn't a love match on either side."

"Oh." Gere frowned at an imagined spot on the glass in his hands. "I almost wish you hadn't told me. I'd like to think of Risë as being in love. It suits her, doesn't it? You're the one more likely to marry out of practicality – or so I thought."

Amanda would have cried again, if she had any tears left. "I thought you said I was worthy of love," she said, trying to keep her voice light, and failing.

"And you are." Gere rubbed at the ersatz spot. "You're just…no, I'm not saying this right. I just think that when you do marry, it will be out of deep abiding love, and all the practicality that goes with it. There won't be any of this love at first sight, in love to be in love stuff for you."

"Yes, I remember what you said." Amanda rinsed the sponge out and put it on the rack to dry. "Of course, it's a little difficult to wake up one morning and realize you're in love when you aren't around anyone to develop that deep, abiding love."

"Oh, I don't know. Things like that can surprise-"

Her phone rang before he could finish his statement and she went into the living room to pick up her bag. "Hello?"

"Amanda? Are you all right?" It was Risë and she didn't sound husky and teary eyed as Amanda expected.

"I'm fine," Amanda hedged. "What about you?"

"I'm fine, too. I called to apologize about what happened this morning. I know-"

"You're not the one who needs to apologize," Amanda interrupted. Gere came through the dining room and raised brows at this statement.

Risë ignored her. "I know you went to a lot of trouble to make everything special for me. No sister could have done more. Stephen was completely out of line to say things the way he said them, but I don't think the content was that far off. If something hasn't started between you and Gere, it's going to."

"Risë!" Amanda's protest was half indignation and half guilt.

"Please," Risë scoffed, "I'm the one with two degrees in science. If anyone can recognize chemistry, it's me. And there is chemistry there, believe me. The air is thick with it. Gere looks at you with such possessiveness and longing I'd be hurt if I didn't know he wasn't looking at you as a sister."

"Oh, yes, he does," Amanda insisted. Behind her, Gere was pacing as if he was anxious about the conversation.

"Oh, no, Amanda, and if you can't see it you're blind. I first noticed it the other night when we all went out together. When Gere kissed you, and then let you go, he looked at you with surprise. He might not know it yet, but he is falling in love with you. To be honest," she lowered her voice, "that was another reason I accepted Stephen…to get out of the way."

"Risë, you shouldn't have done that – especially since you're so wrong." Amanda looked over her shoulder and then lowered her own voice. "Love and chemistry are *not* the same thing." Yet, even as she whispered the words she felt an odd and not unpleasant weakening in her knees. Was it possible that Gere really did feel something for her? Was it possible that this was something she wanted?

"Oh, they are for you and Gere." Risë was adamant. "You two are a pair in that regard. For both of you love means commitment, forever and ever and all of that. If it ever occurs to him to take a step he'll propose. And I think," Risë paused to giggle, "you'll accept."

"You're forgetting something, aren't you?" Amanda said, forcing words out almost soundlessly. "What about Kuwait?"

"Oh, I meant to tell you!" Risë exclaimed. "That's not Gere's baby." She didn't even try to keep her comments hushed. "It's Stephen's. What do you think about that? I'm a wife and a mother!"

"He told you?" Amanda gasped.

"Of course he did. We're married, and he thought I had a right to know. He's not the total snake you two think he is." Risë sighed. "All right, I've played big sister for the first and only time. Get off the phone, look Gere in the eyes and tell him the following: I am not your sister. Then see what he does." There was a click and then silence as she ended the connection.

"Well?" Gere demanded.

Amanda put her phone back into her bag, bemusedly. "Stephen apparently has come clean. He told her about the baby."

Gere sagged against the wall between the living room and dining room. "How did she take it? Is she all right? Does she want to come home?"

"No, big brother, she's fine." The expression sounded funny to her ears now.

Risë had correctly identified her confused feelings. She was in love with Gere, she had probably been for years. If only she was correct about his feelings. "She was actually very pragmatic about it. She laughed and said now she was a wife and mother."

"What else did she say?" he asked, following her back into the kitchen, where she found herself trapped by his piercing stare and her own swirl of hope and denial.

"Not much," she hedged. "She apologized for the outburst this morning."

"She wasn't the one to apologize," he said bitterly. "O'Hara is the one who should have apologized."

"She thinks you should have apologized, too. She didn't so much disagree with what he said, just how he said it."

"What is that supposed to mean? Does she think…"

Amanda faced him squarely, drawing a deep breath for courage. This was the turning point in her life. She would end up with a lifetime of love and security or be packing her bags in twenty minutes. "She told me to give you the following message, from me to you: I am not your sister."

"I know you're not my sister, but-" he stopped, and looked at her again. His eyes widened. He licked his lips, searched for words and finding none stared at her, stunned. "You're not my sister," he repeated, taking a step closer to her. He reached out, hesitantly to touch her shoulder, and then slide his hand around her neck. "You're not my sister," he said again, with more confidence. He pulled her against him. "But you are a very attractive, loving, sweet, intelligent woman." He kissed her closed eyes. "You're the kind of woman a man waits his whole life to find. I've had you a whole lifetime and not even realized it." With his other hand, he lifted her chin and kissed her lips.

Amanda wanted to resist, to remind herself that this man was her guardian/father/brother/ landlord and not a potential lover, but within his arms, his lips against hers, all she could do was remember that he had been the lighthouse for every stormy sea in her life. He was the epitome of safety, and belonging and feeling cared for. He was everything that meant love to her. Risë was right.

Gere held her tight, murmuring things that she didn't understand, but definitely could comprehend. His body shuddered against hers, full of emotion. "Amanda, Amanda," he sighed, lifting his face from her hair. "Tell me that you understand what I feel? Tell me you feel something even kind of, sort of, like it?"

"Oh, I do understand."

He pulled back enough to study her face, anxiously. "And…how do you feel?"

"I love you," she confessed bravely. She had never said that to anyone, not even the boys that she experimented with in the process of growing up. "I guess I always have."

"I don't know when I first loved you." He wrapped his arms around her, as if afraid to let her go. "I only know that while I was kid- while I was away, and I thought I was never going to see you again, I thought about your smile, your voice, the smell of your shampoo, the way you sing when you don't know anyone's around, your practical nature, your sense of humor, your compassion, the way you look after Risë. All those things kept me going every day, kept me determined not to give up, determined to get home.

"And then I did see you and I realized how easy it was to lose everything and everyone that ever mattered; I've been more miserable than I have ever been in my entire life. And I didn't have the words to explain why. Amanda." He released her and backed away. "I'm not sure what I have to offer that you want or need from me, but anything…anything I have is yours. My home, my money, my name…anything you want, take it."

'My name'. Amanda closed her eyes and tried to imagine her name linked with his the way girls often wiled away a boring class by practicing married signatures. Amanda Jeanne Mackie. She liked it. She smiled as she opened her eyes. "I want everything. I'm greedy."

He looked around the kitchen as if in search of some symbolic thing to present to her. Finding nothing, he dropped to his knees, reached for her hands, and pressed them to his lips. "Amanda, are you saying you would marry me?"

"Yes." Her voice broke with tears of joy. She had never cried in happiness before. It was a wonderful sensation.

He stood and kissed her again, but this time it was a different kiss; it was hard, passionate and hungry. He backed away quickly, putting space between them. "I'm sorry. That had nothing to do with what happened over there. I think I've wanted to do that for years," he confessed. He ran his hands through his hair as he looked around the kitchen again. "This has been the damnedest day, hasn't it? You know, this wasn't a very romantic place to propose, but I don't have much experience with that kind of thing."

Amanda looked around the kitchen that had always signified home to her. "Oh, yes it was, Gere. You have no idea how perfect it was."

From somewhere in Gere's room, they could hear his phone ringing.

Amanda laughed. "That will be Risë wanting to know if I followed her instructions."

Gere blushed. "Probably. Do you want to tell her or shall I?"

"You tell her. She called you. She wants to hear it from you."

"She's your sister, too. She always has been. And now it will be official." His phone stopped ringing, and a moment later Amanda's phone began to chime. "Patient she is not." He reached into Amanda's briefcase and pulled out her phone. "Hello?" He listened for a moment. "Risë, you have got to stop meddling in other people's lives. Do you know what you did just now? You made me propose to Amanda."

Even Amanda could hear her squeal of delight.

"I don't know," he said a few minutes later. "I don't intend to sneak off to Reno, that's for sure. Amanda's going to have the whole scenario: white dress, flowers, all her friends. Do you think he'll let you fly back here to be her matron of honor?" He looked across the room at Amanda and mouthed, 'Is that okay with you?'

Amanda nodded. It made things even more perfect.

Gere hung up the phone and pulled her into his arms for a swing around room hug. When he set her down, he found himself looking at the photo montage on the wall. "I'm afraid," he said, nodding toward the pictures, "that our wedding will attract some media attention."

Amanda shrugged. "The newsman is the news again. The story of your life."

"Speaking of that...the network is planning a reorganization over the next six months, and I've been offered a post on the Beltway. Could you give up San Francisco to live in the Capitol?"

"Does it mean you won't be flying off to war zones anymore?"

"Not unless you include Congress," Gere said with a chuckle.

Amanda laughed. She had never felt so much like laughing. "I could live anywhere if you promise me I don't ever have to spend another night watching the news and worrying about you."

"It's a deal. I know it means giving up your position at Bond, Walker & Phills but it's my understanding there are a few lawyers in DC. You might be able to squeeze in there."

"Even if I can't, I'm fine with leaving Bond, Walker & Phills after what happened last night."

"I'm glad to hear that." He kissed her again. "Well, I didn't expect the day to go quite in this direction, did you?"

She shook her head. "Do you mind?"

"Mind? I want to go up on the roof and start shouting. I want to Tweet to the world. I want to get a Breaking News alert out on AP. I want to take you out to the most romantic lunch this city can provide."

Amanda felt flush with joy, triumph, even desire. "I don't know, Gere." She smiled coyly "We could probably manage a pretty romantic lunch right here."

He cocked his head, a little grin playing around his lips. "Miss Mackie, you make me blush. I can see that we'd better set that wedding date." His face darkened, the grin vanished, the playful note in his voice flattened. "Even though I rushed into a proposal, we can't rush into a marriage."

Even though it was not what she wanted to hear, Amanda understood that what he said was realistic and, steady girl that she was, she nodded. "I know."

"It's just, with all that's going on in here," he tapped his temple, "I think that adding marriage to the bargain would…you know?"

She nodded again, trying to look encouraging. "It's enough that we know how we feel. And I don't want to marry what you brought back," she explained carefully. "I think we should wait until you've had some time to process and heal."

"Now I will believe you love me." He didn't touch her but he caressed her face with his intent gaze. "If it was just about being in love with love, or the heady emotions of a proposal, you wouldn't think about waiting, you wouldn't think of what was best for me – for both of us." He frowned. "It could take a while."

Amanda's heart was breaking for all that he had experienced and for all that she was feeling. It was a sweet, searing pain. "I know," she said quietly. "But it would be a mistake to make such a drastic change to your life right now."

He settled into a chair. "It's not going to be easy. Sometimes I feel as if I'm holding on to my sanity by one nerve, and sometimes I feel completely empty." He sighed.

"Gere." Amanda reached out impulsively, brushing his hair back from his eyes. "I won't pretend to understand what you're going through, but I can promise you won't go through it alone."

He smiled up at her. "I think knowing that you're waiting for me is going to help. And where am I going to live until then?"

"What do you mean where? This is your house-"

Gere put a gentle hand over her lips. "It's our house. It always has been, but now it will be legal and official, too, even if we moved to D.C." He looked around the kitchen, as if seeing it through her eyes. "I don't think we could give up this place. We'll always need our home."

Amanda merely nodded in agreement, but inside she was sobbing with relief.

Gere continued, "But, with all that's been going on with me, I'd be more comfortable staying somewhere else until I've seen the doc a few more times. I think I mentioned all my emotions are magnified right now."

Amanda blushed and looked away.

He caught her chin and turned her face back to his. "Promise me you won't regret this."

"How can I regret having what I've always wanted?" she whispered.

"I don't know." He shrugged awkwardly. "Everything's happened so fast I think I'm afraid it could disappear just as fast." He looked down at her, solemnly. "I just don't want you to wake up one morning and decide you made a mistake."

Amanda shook her head. "I'm the practical one, remember? I'm the one who's going to get married with deep and abiding love, remember? A very wise man told me that."

"Wise man," Gere scoffed. "If I were a wise man, I would have proposed to you two years ago when I first got the idea."

"Two years? You just said you never realized-"

"I was waxing poetic. It's journalistic license. The truth is, my feelings for you started shifting a couple of years ago."

"Did you love me two years ago?" she teased.

"I certainly had the inklings."

"Oh, then it's good that you didn't ask me then," Amanda smiled sadly. "You told me it takes time if it's going to last. It's better it happened now. I'm glad it happened now. We've both been through enough to know it's what matters to us. Now I think it will last forever."

"Then that's what it will be." He pulled her into his arms. "Is there anymore champagne? I want to drink to forever."

The End

Thank you for reading
You'll Wake Up One Morning

About the Author

Emjae considers herself a professional romantic, but don't call her work romantic fiction. Like everyone else around Inknbeans, she prefers the term contemporary relationship fiction. She started writing fiction for her grandmother more than twenty years ago, and only recently decided to pick up quill and ink and begin again, after toiling far too long as a technical writer.

She lives in a little castle on a hilltop in Southern California with the demanding and indifferent Lord Mogwollen, her collection of tea pots, crochet hooks and coffees from around the world. She is the last living Dodgers fan.

We hope you've enjoyed *You'll Wake Up One Morning*. If you have questions, comments or constructive criticism you can reach Emjae at Emjae@inknbeans.com.

Other titles by Emjae Edwards:

A Plane Proposal
Wife In the Mirror
Learning To Be Irish
Calling All Hearts
No Greater Love
The Lady Must Decline
Cactus & Mistletow
Once in the Moonlight and
Don't Go To Strangers coming 2013

These books are available at Amazon, Smashwords, fine booksellers everywhere and Inknbeans.com.

Fresh Books Brewed Daily